ECHOES FROM THE VALLEY

ECHOES FROM THE VALLEY

VINAY CAPILA

PARTRIDGE
A Penguin Random House Company

To order additional copies of this book, contact
Partridge India
000 800 10062 62
www.partridgepublishing.com/india
orders.india@partridgepublishing.com

To

my mother,

who was born
in the tranquility of the valley

and whose mind never left it

ACKNOWLEDGEMENT

I owe this work to the untiring effort of
my son, Pranav,

who battled through my manuscript
to hammer it into a presentable shape

and, finally,

also designed the beautiful cover for it.

PREFACE

Over a year back, sitting on the banks of the Ganga beyond Rishikesh, my son and I were discussing an article in a magazine that related stories of the tragic exodus of the Pandits from Kashmir over two decades back. Our discussion that day provided to me the seed of an idea that, perhaps, there was still a tale to be told; rather a tale that needed to be told from a different perspective.

My mother was born in Kashmir, and we visited her maternal home frequently during my childhood—and those visits still bring back happy memories. Then, when I got my first job, I was posted to Kashmir and I stayed there for almost seven years, which corresponded with the period that experienced the two Indo-Pakistan wars of 1965 and 1971. In the subsequent four decades I visited the valley off and on, enticed to do so by pleasant memories, and to meet old friends and colleagues—from different religions and different strata of society. I could feel the pendulum of public opinion swing back and forth.

My last visit was a year back when I found, sitting in Delhi, my pen refused to move beyond the first few pages of this story. While in Kashmir, I met an old friend and spent a few days just sitting and listening to stray stories related by him and his friends, covering the period of maximum turmoil. Then, sitting in a tourist hut in Pahalgam, my pen started moving again. It has been a tough year, a struggle to keep the story travelling on track.

I would like to emphasize that though this story has been strung together with the beads of experiences and memories and thoughts that came to my mind, none of the characters are real or representative of true persons. Nor are any of the incidents a depiction of any historical facts, except in the broader context. Any resemblance to real persons is purely coincidental.

Vinay Capila

April 2014

PROLOGUE

Bashir's fingers were numb as he sat on the bund by the river Jhelum. The chill crept up his toes and seeped towards his heart as he sat there wondering where his friends were. Twelve years was a long time—a lifetime. And yet too short a time to forget the madness of the intervening years: the madness that swept over their homes and rent the love that had taken a decade to nurture. Where was Roshan Bhan? Where was Ravi Chandra? His friends of yore, lost to the turmoil that had swamped all their lives in mindless conflict.

Could they roll back the time and erase the agony of those years—cleanse their minds of the evil that had bedeviled them? Alas that that was possible: that wounds could be healed and scars made to vanish with the wave of a magic wand. But that was not the way of the world: not the way life worked. It was easier to wound—infinitely difficult to heal.

Bashir got up from the cement bench in the small park by the river. This is where he had last sat with Roshan those many years back; where he had made a promise: a promise that still came to haunt him in his moments of loneliness.

THE FRIENDS

"Bashir! Bashir, pass!"

The ball came sizzling across the turf to Ravi. He stopped it with his hockey stick and swiveled to his right, weaving between two defenders before pausing to take a look at the rival goal. The goalkeeper was hunching down in anticipation as he looked nervously at the advancing figure. Through the corner of his eye Ravi saw two defenders converging menacingly towards him. He must act quickly. He feinted towards the left, and then, as the goalkeeper swayed slightly to his right in response, Ravi scooped the ball into the top left hand corner of the goal.

"Goal!" The roar rent the air from the crowd on the sidelines. Bashir came running towards Ravi and wrapped him in an ecstatic bear-hug. Then the other players from their team converged on the two and they all collapsed in a heap.

Before they could take their positions again for the re-start of the game, the referee blew the long whistle signaling the end of play. Don Dosco School had again won the final of the inter-school hockey tournament in Srinagar. The trophy was theirs to keep for another year: to adorn the glass fronted cupboard that was prominently and proudly positioned in the center of the Reception of the school office.

Roshan was among the first of the spectators who rushed onto the field to congratulate their schoolmates. He hugged Bashir and Ravi and thumped them on their backs, his pride and adoration glowing on his face. "Wow, *yaars*, you are the best; you are the best" he repeated again and again, unable to control his joy at his friends being the heroes of the game.

Later, after the presentation ceremony was over and Bashir and Ravi had showered and changed their clothes, the trio headed towards Lal Chowk to find a place to hold their own celebration with some hot snacks.

"What a goal *yaar*," Bashir said, his mouth stuffed with *samosa* filling. "You had that goalkeeper completely foxed."

"Ya, but all the credit should go to your beautiful pass Bashir," Ravi responded.

"Didn't I say that before?" Roshan chipped in, "you two are the best! What would the school do without you?"

Having finished their snacks, the three headed for the bund. The Jhelum flowed sluggishly between the houseboats on its sides towards Amira Kadal, the first old bridge that spanned the river, before meandering through the rest of the city. They plonked themselves on the low parapet wall bordering the bund and watched the river flow below them.

"So, another semester before we give our finals," said Ravi, playing with some pebbles, "what are you planning on doing after that Bashir?"

"I don't know yaar," Bashir replied laconically. "My father says enough of studies. He feels that I should just join the family handicrafts business—maybe start another shop in India, in Chandigarh or Delhi, so that we have more steady sale all around the year."

Ravi chewed reflectively on a piece of straw for some time, then said, "But don't you think you should at least go through college? It's a different experience; it will widen your perspective on life. Perhaps you will want to do something totally different after that—not just selling druggets and fur coats and leather gloves. There is a whole new world outside the valley; a whole world offering so much more."

"But if I have to handle my own shop in India, that will be my contact with the whole wide world won't it? I'll gain that wider perspective while I set up the business there. And I don't see any reason why I should work for anyone else when we have our own business."

"True Bashir, but what I meant was . . . never mind," Ravi said.

"I plan to go to college," Roshan said eagerly, trying to cut across the awkward silence that had developed, "I don't have a family business to fall back on, so I'll have to slog a bit. I . . ."

"What do you mean slog a bit," Bashir interrupted angrily. "You think setting up a new shop in India will not involve any hardship? I can tell you that it is not going to be easy. I'll have to work damn hard to get it going."

"Hey, don't get angry, Bashir," Roshan said defensively. "I just meant that I don't have an alternative to going to college. Unless I do that I'll not have the qualifications to get a suitable job. And I have no option to working for someone. So I plan to do B.Com. and then, if my father can afford it, do Chartered Accountancy. I believe that there is a very promising future in that field. Who knows, after getting some experience I might even set up my own practice."

"Good for you," Ravi said. "I'm just thinking of doing a B.A. for the time being. We also have a family business, but my father feels that after graduating I should go to America for doing an M.B.A. After coming back I could start a factory, or set up another firm to diversify our business. But I'm jumping the gun here; it will take a long time for those plans to mature."

"Looks like we are going to part after school," Bashir said, flinging a pebble into the river.

"Not really," Ravi said, thumping his back. "You're not going to get rid of us so soon. It looks like both Roshan and I will do our graduation from A.S. College, since that is the only decent college here. So we will be able to meet almost every day. I'm sure that your father's plans for opening a shop outside the valley will take time to concretize; he will want you to get used to the business—learn the ropes. And who knows, he might still decide that you should finish college before you join the business. Either way, all three of us will keep meeting regularly."

The call of the muezzin from a mosque down river suddenly blared over a loudspeaker. It was time for evening prayers. The three friends decided to leave for their homes, since it would soon be dark.

∞

BOSTON

Ravi tossed and turned in his bed, then finally flung the quilt off and got out. He walked towards the window of his bedroom facing the front yard. He smiled wryly. Yes, he could only call it the front yard, because all his efforts to tame it into a well manicured garden had failed. His house was on the fringe of a forest in the suburbs of Boston. It was actually on the slope of an area carved out of the forest itself, surrounded by maples and firs and pines, with small and large rocks strewn around them, peeping out between bushes and shrubs and grass; a difficult landscape to tame.

Among the trees dotting his yard was a large maple that claimed centre-stage in the sloping non-lawn. Its leaves had turned slowly from green, to yellow, to rust over the past weeks, as the chill crept into the night air with the sun slowly drifting southwards. Ravi had lived here for nearly five years, but, for some reason, this feeling of unease was markedly pronounced this year: a deep feeling of loss, despite the success he had achieved in his job; a feeling that he was missing something—that something was missing.

As he looked out of the window at the orange-rust leaves of the maple, he thought of the chinars back home. 'Back home!' The phrase jolted him. How could he still think of Srinagar as back home? And yet, how could he not! For that was what it was; the place of his birth; the place of his longest, fondest memories; the place that had nurtured him through his long maturing years and moulded his psyche.

They had lived in a large house—a mansion really. The chinars had not been in their front yard, but in the meadow just beyond the road in front of their house—the meadow that stretched for half a kilometer before any structure broke its rolling symmetry. The chinars dotted this meadow and provided shade to the stray jersey cows that grazed there, unmindful of the children shrieking in mock terror as they played their innocent games. Was their mock terror a precursor of what was to come later? No, it could not be! No one could have envisaged that in the idyllic scene that permeated the meadow. And yet . . .

Ravi thought back, wading through the foggy memory that clouded his mind. The change had already started as he grew up—out of childhood into adolescence. The meadow had been violated and an auditorium had sprouted up in front of their house—and beyond that a sports stadium. An eight foot wall cordoned off the area beyond the front road. The vast open spaces of yore were no more. But, by then, Ravi had grown out of the need for those spaces and had entered into the larger space that was the world, a world of new freedoms and new relationships.

School was a new liberating experience for him. He now explored the new spaces that opened up to him; a tentative forming of new relationships that could develop into life-long friendships. But what was life-long? What was a life span? These questions did not spring up at that time. What had been important was the now—the then. The future had a nebulous, distant quality—that could be dreamt, not grasped. But then that was what life had been then: a time for dreaming and chasing rainbows.

JAMMU

Roshan walked through Raghunath Bazar, the searing sun beating mercilessly on his head. It was hot, and the melting coal-tar on the road radiated its own squishy heat. The soles of his shoes seemed to be melting. On both sides of the road the shops had put out their little awnings in a vain effort to ward off the heat. But the hot air crawled under the lips of the awnings to try and escape into the shade; to penetrate the semi-darkness of the tube-lit interiors.

Roshan was tempted for a moment to seek relief in the cool dark interior of one of the shops, but there were mainly clothing shops here, offering saris and other ladies' garments. In between these there were general merchant shops or those with electronic goods; none that could provide an excuse for him to enter and browse around for a while. The occasional *dhabas* and tea shops would be too hot and stuffy to provide any respite. In any case, he should hurry up and reach the bus-stand so that he could catch a bus to take him across the Tawi River to Gandhi Nagar, where he was supposed to meet a potential client. Selling insurance was a hit or miss business—with more misses than hits. The place was crawling with insurance agents. He had to keep plodding to try and eke out a living.

Unlike Raghunath Bazar, the bus stand was bustling with activity even in the fierce afternoon heat. He hopped on to a bus with a Gandhi Nagar tag pasted on its brow, and found a window seat away from the sun; at least he would get some breeze once the bus moved downhill. Another ten minutes and they were crossing the old Tawi bridge. The river below was only that in name; not even a rivulet—more of a drain, for that was all that remained of it till the rains came to flush it out and give it an iota of respectability.

As the bus crawled over the bridge in the heavy traffic, Roshan thought of that other river—which had been the lifeline of their city those many years ago; which was still the lifeline of that city he was sure, but he could no longer claim it to be his city. How could that be, he wondered, that a place that was the place of his birth; the place whose breath nurtured him to maturity; the place where he received his education and formed his dearest friendships; was no longer his—not of his own volition, but with crass imposition? And the river that he had always thought of as his river had floated away out of his grasp, to leave him staring at this turbid drain flowing under the hot steel girder bridge.

The bus moved on as his eyes misted over with the subdued sigh that escaped his dry lips.

A TREK

The finals were over; two months to wait for the results, and before they could chalk out their future course of action. Bashir was still undecided whether he should enter college before he joined his father's business, or take the plunge straight away. Or rather, his father was undecided, for Bashir had a minimal say in the matter. He himself vacillated on his choice from day to day. His friends constantly urged him to taste the freedom and excitement of college life before he tied himself up to the life-long drudgery of making money. His father wondered whether sixteen was not too tender an age for him to start working on opening a new branch outside the valley—away from home. Perhaps it was better that he go to college and work in the evenings at their Srinagar shop to gain some experience? As far as Ravi and Roshan were concerned, they just had to wait to see how they had fared in their exams, and whether their results would get them admissions into the courses they wanted to join in college.

Most evenings the three friends met on the left bund of the Jhelum, near the Convent School, from where they could sit and watch the activity on the other side where all the shops and restaurants were located. Sometimes they would take a *shikara* and cross the river—to go for a snack, or just stroll around Residency Road or Lal Chowk.

One day, walking through Maisuma Bazar, Ravi said, "This is getting so boring *yaar*, why don't we go to Pahalgam for a few days? We could even go for a small trek up the Lidar valley to the Kolhai glacier. Once the results are out we will be caught up in so much activity that we will not get any opportunity to go out for a long time."

"That's a good idea," Bashir said excitedly. "It will be a good experience, the trek. I'll have to check if my father will agree. It is not the tourist season, and even though he insists that I go to the shop during the morning, we are just sitting around doing nothing, or walking up and down the street sunning ourselves."

Roshan looked less enthusiastic. "I don't know, father might not like the idea. Won't it be a lot of expense staying in Pahalgam—and if we go on this trek?"

"Don't worry about the expense Roshan," Ravi said. "Its off season, so everything will be cheaper. We can always find a room to stay in at the Tourist Reception Centre, or some cheap accommodation. We just need one room, and I will pay for that. And as far as the trek is concerned, we can take along our sleeping bags and haversacks and some canned food. We can always spend the nights with shepherds in their huts along the way. It's only a four day trek, to the base of the glacier and back. With a couple of days in Pahalgam it should not be too expensive."

"I don't know *yaar*," Roshan said, "I don't like the idea of sponging off you chaps. Let me see if I can convince my father to part with some money, so that I can share some of the expense."

"You do that, but even otherwise, you shouldn't get so sensitive," Ravi cajoled. "It'll be such fun, spending a week together. Just convince your father to give you sufficient money for the bus fare to Pahalgam and back—and some *daal roti* costs for the trip, to ease your conscience. Bashir and I will take care of the rest."

"Yes," put in Bashir, "what are friends for. And as Ravi said, we might not get such an opportunity for a long time to come once the results are out and we get involved with so many other things."

And, on that note, they parted for the night.

∞

The bus had an unhealthy cough, and it seemed to be reluctant to leave the shelter of the bus stand. But the driver was persistent and kept pumping on the accelerator till the cough converted to a deep throated groan and black smoke spewed out of the back. Then with a gnashing of gears it moved onto Residency Road, spluttering a few last farewells to its sleeping companions at the stand. Ravi and Bashir and Roshan let out a triumphant cry of victory and thumped each other on the shoulders, as if the fact of the movement of the bus were a major achievement.

It was a week since they had first thought up the plan for their little holiday cum trek: a week of feverish lobbying with their families to permit them to go on the trip. Well, not so much for Ravi, since his father was all for adventurous ventures that involved physical effort. 'Builds your character', he would say. But he wanted to have details of who his companions would be on the trip. Ravi gave him brief details.

"Oh, Shafiq Ahmed's son, from Ahmed Joy & Sons on Linking Road," he said. "I know Shafiq Ahmed. He is a member of the Kashmir Chamber of Commerce. A bit aggressive in the Chamber meetings, but that is okay. Most of these Muslim traders of handicrafts are like that. But who is this Bhan?"

Ravi gave him the sketchy information he had.

"Okay, so his father has a *kirana* shop, a provisions store, in Maisuma Bazar. Do they also live there? You know, we used to have a house there ourselves a long time back, before we built this one," his father said.

"They have their own house in Habba Kadal, father," Ravi answered, not knowing which way his father's thoughts were flying.

"Well, okay. I suppose it is okay for you to go, since they are both classmates from Don Dosco," his father said hesitantly. Ravi gave a sigh of relief.

∞

Shafiq Ahmed was reluctant. "What's all this trekking frekking Bashir? Here I am waiting for your school results, in order to decide what you are going to do next, and you want to go off for a holiday with your friends? You should start spending more time at the shop, so that you can get some idea of our trade. It makes no sense going for a holiday before you have even started work. Have you ever seen me going off on holidays—except occasionally when we go to Chasma Shahi or Nishat gardens for a picnic?"

"O, let him go," Bashir's mother called out from the next room. "He has been studying so hard for his examinations. Let him have a little fun before you plunge him into your work. As it is the poor boy is looking so lost, not knowing how his life is going to shape up. I feel you should let him join college; let him enjoy life a little. He has a whole life-time to do your work."

"You keep out of this Sameena," Shafiq retorted, "you are bent on spoiling the boy. As it is I can't make up my mind on what to do with him. Let us see how the results come. If he gets a first division, I might just decide to let him go to college, otherwise it is pointless. What we are talking about at this time is this new scheme of his: this trekking shrekking with his friends, and you are bringing other issues into the discussion. Who are these friends of yours anyway, Bashir?"

Bashir gathered some courage, looking gratefully at the door from which his mother's support had floated out, and blurted, "They are both classmates from school. We have been together all these years. One is Ravi Chandra. His father has that big business selling construction and hardware products and they have a big house in Wazir Bagh. The other one is Roshan Bhan. His father has a *kirana* shop in Maisuma Bazar and they live in Habba Kadal."

"Chandra . . . Chandra," his father muttered, trying to dig into his memory for where he had heard the name before. Then, "Oh, yes, he must be the son of that Ramdev Chandra, that pumped up fool. He thinks he is the king of Kashmir ever since he became the President of the Kashmir Chamber of Commerce. I make sure that I pull him down a peg or two every time we have a Chamber meeting. He is harmless enough otherwise. But this Bhan chap, you say his father has a *kirana* shop in Maisuma? Do you think he is the right company for you?"

"He is one of the brightest students in class, father," Bashir put in quickly. "He is the one who helped me a lot with my mathematics problem. He is planning to do B.Com in college and then Chartered Accountancy. He could be a great help to me when I join business."

"Well, in that case . . ." his father said reluctantly. "But I hope everyone is paying for their own costs. I don't want you subsidizing anyone's trip. I know the Chandra boy can pay for himself, but this *kirana* merchant's son . . ."

"Of course, father," Bashir interrupted quickly, before his father could think of any excuse to go back on his decision.

∽

As Roshan had anticipated, his father was totally against the idea. He felt that it was a total waste of time. In any case he did not have money to throw away on such excursions.

"You take a bus and go to the Mughal Gardens," he said. "Or go for a walk along the Boulevard on Dal Lake. Thousands of tourists come from all over the world just to do that. And if you are so fond of trekking, go around the Dal and Nagin lakes and back here—I am sure that it will be a good eight or ten kilometers. Why go all the way to Pahalgam for doing it. There are enough mountains near Srinagar for you to climb, if that is what you want to do."

But Roshan had an ace up his sleeve that he used sparingly when he had run into the wall of resistance put up by his father, and he knew that this was the occasion to use it. He went to his *mama*, his maternal uncle, who was capable of turning his brother-in-law's intransigent decisions into a ball of pliable putty. And that's what happened. Next morning his father called him into his room and handed him a thin wad of money, gruffly saying that he had changed his mind for this once; but Roshan would have to pay back that money by helping him with his accounts at the *kirana* shop for a month after his return. And no loose spending he added sternly.

❀

Well, all's well that begins well, they all thought as the bus rumbled out of Srinagar—beyond Broadway cinema on the right and beyond the cantonment. The Jhelum river appeared momentarily, shimmering sleepily in the morning light, as they topped a slight slope—and then was left behind. The bus stopped briefly at Pampore to take in more passengers, and the boys scampered out to buy some *bakkarkhanis*: the sweet or salty Kashmiri crusty bread that served as great snacks with tea, or even as delicious anytime munchies for ravenous boys.

It was early morning and the breeze was cold, sneaking through the gaps in the window frames. The sun had made a late entry on the scene, peeping weakly through the misty horizon. The boys had already taken out a sweet *bakkarkhani* each; just to sample it they assured each other. The excitement and joy of their outing was coursing through them.

"Look! Saffron fields," Roshan shouted excitedly, as the bus topped a slope and entered a plateau. The road pierced the plateau, straight as an arrow. On both sides lay the rolling fields of saffron, stretching to the horizon. Far on the right, almost lost in the haze, they could see the high mountain range capped with snow. They watched the scene, entranced, as they nibbled at their *bakkarkhanis*. All too soon the road dipped out of the plateau and wended its way through the fields shorn of their paddy crop.

"Wow, what a scene that was!" Ravi said in an awestruck voice. "I've seen it a number of times, but it still stuns me every time I pass through here in this season."

"Ya, me too," Bashir mumbled. "You know, I once came here on a moonlit night when the saffron flowers were in full bloom; the whole countryside was a luminescent purple in that light. It was awesome."

"Too good *yaar*," Roshan added. "No wonder they call our Kashmir like heaven on earth. We are so lucky to be born here—to live here."

They sat there, munching their *bakkarkhanis* and drinking in the beauty of the countryside, too overcome for further conversation.

∞

It was ten-thirty by the time the bus reached Mattan, and they were feeling ravenous despite their constant munching on the *bakkarkhanis*. The driver said that he would stop there for fifteen minutes to have his breakfast.

He suggested the passengers do the same, or go and visit the small Hindu shrine the village was famous for. The boys were happy to get off and stretch their legs, and to have some tea and butter toast.

While they were having their tea and toast Bashir asked, "How come there is this old Hindu shrine out here. And who are all these pandeys swarming around?"

"Why, this is as old as Shankracharya temple in Srinagar," replied Roshan.

"Or Kheerbhavani shrine near Ganderbal," Ravi added. "They have all been here for ages—even before the Mughals invaded the valley. And the pandeys are just as old an institution; they are like record keepers of many Hindu families. I am sure one of them would have records of my family. Do you want me to demonstrate?"

"No, no," Bashir said impatiently, "in any case the bus is ready to go.

As if on cue, the driver started blowing the horn and they quickly hopped on. Moving out of Mattan they were soon on a road that moved parallel to a turbulent stream, frothing white where it tumbled over boulders. On the other side the mountain closed in on them till the road curved along its base, meandering up the valley, which got narrower and narrower till it burst into the expanse of Pahalgam valley. The bus turned right onto a wide open square piece of land that served as the bus-stand.

Even though it was off-season, a crowd of coolies and hotel agents and pony owners swarmed around the bus, clamouring for custom. The boys got out of the bus and Roshan quickly clambered up the steel ladder at the back. He sorted out their haversacks and sleeping bags and passed them down to Ravi and Bashir. Strapping their belonging on their backs they went out towards the main road, waving aside the agents and coolies who still followed them.

The Tourist Reception Centre was the first big structure at the entrance of Pahalgam, adjacent to the bus-stand, and the boys decided to check if they could get accommodation there. It would be the cheapest, clean accommodation they would find in Pahalgam, if they were lucky. Being off-season, they didn't have any problem getting a room, and they dumped their baggage in it and went out to find a *dhaba* for their lunch. It was surprising how soon they could get hungry. The crisp air and the excitement of the journey probably contributed to it to a large extent.

Walking up the gentle slope of the main Pahalgam bazaar road they could see that some of the shops were already closed, since the tourist season had ended and winter was approaching. In the center of the bazaar they came across the 'Punjabi Dhaba', which seemed to be the most prominent low cost eatery on the street. They looked at each other with questioning glances, trying to determine if anyone had any objections: on whether this was acceptable to all of them.

"I don't have any problems about halaal or haraam," Bashir said, "if that is what you are trying to ask. And I don't have to relate everything we did to my father on my return. So let's go."

"I don't eat any meat in any case," Ravi put in, "so no problem. I am told that the vegetarian food here is really tasty."

"Yes," said Roshan mischievously, "I believe they make the daal-sabzi even tastier when they dig the same ladle into them as they use for the chicken korma pot."

They entered the *dhaba*, laughing loudly, and ordered their selection of dishes. In deference to Ravi's vegetarian status they ordered only vegetarian dishes, so that they could all share them. After finishing their meal they walked across the *maidaan* to the Lider river. They sat on its bank, watching the sparkling stream rushing by, tumbling over the rocks.

"How peaceful it is here," Bashir said. "Thank God we came at this time of the year. In the tourist season this place is crammed with those noisy Indians with their shrieking brats. I came once in summer, to bring some parcels that my father wanted to deliver to a shop here, and I did not want to stay more than that one day once I had come across those crowds."

"Hey, what do you mean by 'those noisy Indians'," Ravi retorted. "We are Indians too; and most children shriek when they are happy and excited. Didn't you, when you were younger and went out for family picnics with other kids?"

"You know what I mean *yaar*," Bashir responded. "We are different, we are Kashmiri. We don't shout and scream like those tourists from India."

"Except when you form processions and shout slogans," Ravi interrupted tersely. "And anyway, how can you be resentful of the tourists, noisy or not, when they are the ones who sustain your livelihood. Without them you wouldn't have any business. Without . . ."

"Forget it!" Bashir retorted angrily. "If India were to leave us alone we could become like Switzerland."

"You mean that if the terrorists were to leave us alone," Ravi put in angrily.

"The terrorists are here because India won't leave. They want to help us get our freedom. They are here to terrorize the Indian army and police into leaving."

"That's not true. They are here because Pakistan wants to take us over; and when they tried to do it openly twice earlier, they got beaten into pulp. So now they do it like cowards—in the guise of infiltrators trained to kill in the dark. They . . ."

"Hey, hey, hey! Hold on," Roshan interrupted. "Who is shouting now? The two of you are fighting like cocks; making more noise than any tourists. At least the tourists make noise out of joy—happy noise—you are making angry noise, disturbing the peace and tranquility of this place."

"Sorry, sorry," Ravi said sheepishly. "You are right, this is a pointless argument. After all we are all friends—one family."

"Ya," Bashir grunted in a subdued tone. "Let's get back to the market and buy some provisions for our trek."

∞

The next morning they had an early, light breakfast and checked out of the Tourist Center. They had bought some tins of condensed milk and baked beans and cheese and bread and biscuits from a provision store on the main street the previous evening. Along with the *bakkarkhanis* left over from their purchase in Pampore, they had sufficient emergency rations in case they did not find any suitable eating places on their short trek. They had decided that their first stop would be Aru, about twelve kilometers away, where they were told there was a tourist bungalow for an overnight stay.

From the end of the main bazaar they followed a narrow, rough path down to the *maidaan*. Traversing a few short wooden bridges across dried up rivulets, they headed towards the end of the main Pahalgam valley. From there they followed the road that ran along the Lidar river. The air was crisp and cold and they made steady progress even with the weight of the haversacks and sleeping bags on their backs. They chatted excitedly among themselves and occasionally Roshan burst into song—a mish-mash of Hindi and Kashmiri words strung together by him and floated on popular Bollywood film tunes.

After an hour and a half their pace began to flag and they decided to take a break. Unhitching their haversacks from their backs, they sat down on some boulders by the side of the road. The river had taken its own route and the road was now only a rough jeep-able track. The forest around them was not very thick and consisted of mainly coniferous trees with sparse undergrowth here and there. They decided that a *bakkarkhani* each would help them to recuperate the energy they had expended traversing the last five kilometers. They sat munching them for about ten minutes and then downed them with sips of water from their water bottles. Then they again hoisted the haversacks on their backs and started trudging along the path.

The going was a little tougher now: the road rolling up and down the humps in the mountain as it climbed into the higher region that would lead them into the valley that formed the base into which the Kolhai glacier descended. Somewhere below them, hidden by the trees, they could hear the faint roar of the river. They stopped more frequently as the day progressed, their bodies unaccustomed to long treks with backpacks. However, their stops were shorter except for the hour they gave themselves for a lunch—of cheese and tomato sandwiches that they had brought along—munched by the side of a small brook that bubbled down a slope in the mountain before disappearing into some bushes.

It was nearly dusk when they finally reached Aru, where they had planned to stop over for the night. To their surprise, however, Aru was no tourist resort—or even a large village. All they could see was a smattering of wooden huts strung along a narrow path leading down the valley. There was also a larger wooden hut that advertised itself as a tourist bungalow, with a little signboard in one corner. Even that was closed and shuttered, except for a small smoke blackened room at the back that was obviously the caretaker's quarters.

They unhitched their haversacks and plonked them on the narrow porch fronting the hut; then stood wondering what to do. The sun had already disappeared behind the mountain on their left, but they could see its dying rays glistening golden on the ice clad peak far down the valley on what was probably the mountain down which the Kolhai glacier descended. In the valley itself they could see a number of streams flowing down gentle slopes, to meet the larger stream that disappeared into the trees around a bend in the valley. In the far distance they could spot some sheep crawling around a meadow, munching at grass near a cluster of rough tents. It was probably a temporary camp of the *bakkarwals* or *gujjars*, the nomadic shepherds migrating out of the higher mountains, seeking fresh pastures for their sheep before the winter set in.

They had been sitting on the steps of the porch, watching this scene for about half an hour, when the caretaker of the 'tourist bungalow' finally made his appearance. He was quite taken aback on seeing them sitting there, since no tourists came here this late in the year. Bashir explained to him in Kashmiri that they were all from a school in Srinagar and had decided to do a little trekking in the mountains before joining college. The caretaker, whose name was Gulam Ali, said that he was not allowed to open any rooms for visitors unless they had a permit from their office in Pahalgam, but since they were Kashmiri students, and would only be staying overnight, he would open one room for them on the side. However, they should not tell anyone about this, otherwise he would be in trouble.

Assured of shelter for the night, they were all more relaxed. They put their haversacks in the room opened for them and took out their sleeping bags for spreading on the one large wooden double-bed that lay in the center of the room. Then, putting on their windcheaters, they went to Gulam Ali's room at the back of the bungalow, with a can of baked beans and a loaf of bread and the small tin plates and mugs they had carried with them. They hoped that they would be able to warm the beans in Gulam Ali's fireplace and have their dinner in his hopefully cosier room.

Gulam Ali's room was blackened with soot, since it also served as his kitchen. There was a wood-fired fireplace-cum-cooking stove with a chimney in the wall opposite to the door opening into the room. Next to the door was a window, which was shuttered with wooden slats. On one side was a small wooden cot with some bed clothes and a quilt piled on one side. Above it, from nails driven into the wall, hung some clothes.

Gulam Ali had lit a fire in the stove with some chopped sticks and logs and placed a tin cooking pot on top. The chimney was obviously not too effective since some of the smoke from the fire was already trickling over the lip of the chimney front and spilling over into the room. It rose to the ceiling and formed a grey cloud in the orange light from the wood fire that illuminated the room.

"Come in Sahib, come in," Gulam Ali waved to the boys, seeing them peering in through the partly open door. He spread out a reed mat on the floor next to a side wall, for them to sit on. "I have just started cooking some rice and *kadam saag* for my dinner. Would you like me to make some extra for you? You must be very hungry after your long walk through the day."

"Thank you, Gulam Ali," Ravi responded, "but we would just like to heat our can of beans after you have finished cooking; and we have plenty of bread to go with the beans. Of course we would like to sit here with you while we all have our food, if it is no trouble for you?"

"It will be an honour for me," Gulam Ali replied. "Perhaps I will have the honour of making a meal for you on your way back? If I know in advance, I could make some meat curry for you to go with the rice?"

"Thank you for the offer, Gulam Ali," Bashir replied. "But Ravi bhai is vegetarian, so no meat. But we will definitely have some rice and *kadam saag* curry with you on the way back, Insha'Allah!"

They sat on the reed mat, their backs to the rough plastered sooty wall, chatting while they waited for Gulam Ali's rice to cook. They had placed their can of baked beans near the base of the fire stove, where there was sufficient heat for it to warm up in ten-fifteen minutes.

"So, Gulam Ali, how long have you been here, looking after this tourist bungalow?" Roshan asked.

"I have been here ever since this place was built some years back," he replied, poking the sticks in the stove to keep the fire going, and turning their tin around so that it would get heated evenly from all sides. "I am from a village up on the mountain on the left. I used to tend to some goats and sheep there. But when they started building this tourist bungalow, I thought it would be good to have a government job and a steady income—however small that might be. So I left my village and asked my brother to tend to the animals, and came here."

"You don't have any other family? You are not married?" Ravi asked.

"I was married some years back, when I was in my village," Gulam Ali replied, looking into the fire. "She was very young, and beautiful. But she died in child-birth with our first child. Perhaps she was too young to be a mother; perhaps God had other plans for her and took her away." He sat, poking the sticks into the fire, reminising. A little wry smile played on his lips, his face lit up by the orange glow of the fire. An uneasy silence descended upon the group for some time; then Gulam Ali raised the lid of the pot and peered through the steam that escaped. "The rice seems to be ready," he said, taking the pot off the fire with the help of a rag.

Bashir sprang forward to touch the can. "Our beans seem to be warm enough as well," he said. "Let's open the can. Come on boys, lay out the plates so that I can pour the baked beans into them." He looked at Gulam Ali and inquired, "Would you like to taste some of the beans as well?"

"Just a little, sahib, just to see the taste; otherwise I have more than sufficient of my *bhaa*t and *kadam*. Perhaps you would like to taste some of that as well? There is enough."

They unwrapped the loaf of bread and then all of them shared out the strange mixture of beans and bread and rice and the leafy vegetable curry prepared by Gulam Ali. Somehow the spicy *kadam* and the tangy beans made an interesting combination and they soon polished off the stuff on their plates and had second helpings. Then licking their fingers they went outside the room. They had noticed a large drum with a tap at the bottom, mounted on a brick platform just outside the room. They washed their hands and their plates from the tap, then went inside again to warm their cold hands near the fire. After a little while they bid farewell to Gulam Ali for the night.

"Thank you, Gulam Ali," Ravi said. "We must go to our room now; it is getting cold and we are very tired from our day of walking. We plan to start on our onward journey just after daybreak, so that we can reach Lidarwat by the afternoon. Then we can go to the base of the Kolhai glacier the next day and return to Aru by that evening. So we hope to see you then—and perhaps we can share your tasty *bhaat* and *kadam* again then?"

"Don't worry sahib," Gulam Ali responded with a smile. "I will be up before dawn and will prepare tea for you before you leave; and I will certainly prepare a meal for you the night after next."

∞

Roshan was walking down the road towards his house when he heard a loud rumble of approaching trucks. Far down the road he could see a cloud of dust and then some police trucks emerged from it. In the large manhole type opening on top of the cab of the leading truck stood a helmeted policeman with a stengun in his hands resting on top of the cab roof and pointed down the road. Suddenly, from behind Roshan, there materialised a crowd of young boys. Most of them were wearing faded jeans and *phirans* on top. Their hands were tucked inside the deep pockets of their *phirans*. As the convoy of trucks drew near, the hands emerged from the pockets, holding tennis ball size stones, which they started lobbing at the approaching police trucks. The stones clattered loudly as they hit the steel sides of the trucks. The policeman on the cab of the truck opened fire with his stengun. The noise of the crackling gun fire and the clatter of stones against the trucks grew louder by the moment.

Roshan felt as if he was falling into a ditch, his hands clamped to his ears in terror. Then all other noises faded and there was only a loud banging. Roshan woke up with a start. He was disoriented. Where was he? It was dark all around him, but the banging continued. Then, above the noise there was a voice shouting, "Sahib, wake up, it is dawn. I am preparing some tea for all of you."

Roshan quickly unzipped himself out of his sleeping bag and got out to go and open the door. The sharp morning chill that had crept into the room had him fully awake in a moment. Behind him he could hear two groggy voices enquiring about what was happening and complaining about the noise.

"Get up sleepy heads," he called over his shoulder, "Gulam Ali is here to get us going. He says he will soon have tea ready for us." He unbolted the door and thanked Gulam Ali for waking them up, and told him that they should be able to leave within half an hour after they had washed up and re-packed their bags.

Soon they were all packed and ready to go. They kept their haversacks on the little porch outside their room and went to Gulam Ali's room at the back to have some tea and biscuits before they started their journey for the day. It was very cold outside and there was just a faint glow of daylight over the top of the mountain on their right. A heavy mist covered the ground down the valley. The path they had to travel on disappeared into the mist some two hundred yards away. It was deathly still—not even the morning twitter of birds broke the silence that shrouded them.

Gulam Ali's room was suffused with the golden glow of the fire that burnt in his hearth. He looked up at them as they entered and took down the pot in which the tea had been brewing over the fire. "Right on time," he said smiling a welcome at them, "the tea is ready, and I have some Kashmiri *kulchas* for you to take along with it. You will need the extra energy for traveling in this cold."

He poured out the tea into the mugs they held out for him to fill, and slid a tin plate heaped with *kulchas* towards them. They cradled the hot mugs in their hands to thaw out their chilled fingers, then dipped the brittle dry *kulchas* into the hot tea before slurping the soggy remains into their mouths.

After a while Ravi drained the last of the tea out of his mug and said, "Thank you, Gulam Ali. If it hadn't been for this hot tea and the *kulchas*, we would not have been able to drum up enough courage to proceed on our journey. But tell me, this path leading down from the front of the bungalow, do we just follow that all the way, or can you give us some additional directions to follow?"

"You just go down the path, sahib, till you come to a fork in the road. Take the path on the left—it goes a little uphill and into the trees. Though that road is longer, it is more firm and has a number of log bridges fording the small streams that come down the mountains. The path on the right actually goes straight down the valley, but on that you have to cross the streams with icy cold water—and unless the bakkarwals have made little crossings for themselves by putting stones or rocks into the streams, it would be very difficult and even dangerous for you to cross them. So, even though that is the shorter route, it is very much tougher to travel on, especially for you, who are not accustomed to such terrain. Either way, you should be able to reach Lidderwat by noon, or just after. Ask for Gul Mohammad out there and give him my reference; he will be able to help you with arranging a room for the night, and for some tea and hot food if you need some."

The boys thanked Gulam Ali again and gave him some money for all the trouble he had taken. Then, hitching their haversacks onto their backs, they headed down the path, stamping their feet to restore circulation into their cold toes.

Despite their windcheaters and warm woolen socks and gloves and caps they were chilled to the bone as they walked into the misty morning. However, they started off at a slow jog and the chill began to drain out of their bodies, even though their noses still dribbled with the cold air that struck their faces. Roshan again struck up his lilting Kashmiri folk song and Ravi and Bashir joined him in a cheerful chorus. The mist receded in front of them, as if pushed back by the stridency of their song. The glow of sunlight was slowly becoming brighter, even though there was no sign of the sun itself.

In about half an hour they came to the fork in the road that Gulam Ali had talked about. They stopped to regain their breath and to decide which route they should take. The path on the left would take them up the slope and into the tree-line: the safer and easier road according to Gulam Ali. The path a little to the right was the shorter though more difficult one. From what they had seen last evening, it seemed the more scenic path once the mist had cleared; running along the valley and through the camp of the bakkarwals with their herds of sheep and goats. In their moment of indecision the latter seemed more alluring—adventurous and with the possibility of chatting with the bakkarwals. What were they like? What sort of life did they live? Their life seemed to be a poetic existence shrouded in mystery: an element of mysticism.

"Let's take the path that goes straight through the valley," Roshan said as they sat on some boulders at the side. "I am sure that the mist will lift soon, and we might just get some warmth from the sunlight once the sun makes its appearance."

"But what about the streams that we will have to cross on the way?" Ravi interjected with a tone of doubt. "And I am sure that the grass on the meadows will be wet with the night's dew; we will get our shoes and socks all wet, which is not a very welcome proposition in this cold weather. Besides who knows when the sun will come out?"

"I'm okay either way," Bashir put in, "but I feel the trek through the valley might be more adventurous and romantic—walking through the misty meadows and crossing the frothing streams. The streams, in any case, can't be very wide, emerging down the mountain at this time of the year. We could always build our own stepping stones for crossing them as we go along. It will actually be much more fun than just tramping along the path through the trees."

"We could also talk to the bakkarwals, when we go through their camp down the valley," Roshan put in eagerly. "I've always found them very fascinating; nomads living under the blue skies: masters of their own world."

"Well, you two seem to be determined to take the tough route," Ravi said reluctantly, "so I am out-voted and we have to take the plunge. At least you won't be able to blame me if one of you takes an unscheduled dip in an icy cold stream."

They shrugged their haversacks onto their backs again and carried on the narrower path that led through the mist covered valley.

Far above them on the left, through the trees bordering the regular path they should normally have taken, hawk eyes watched their progress passively. 'Boys! Just young boys out for adventure; not really worthy of sacrifice—or ransom. But, who knows? If they had followed the upper path, it might have been worthwhile finding out. It might just have been good sport to . . . well, never mind, we have more serious plans to execute once we are nearer the villages to the south.' Gul Bux motioned to his companions scattered under the trees, awaiting his instructions. They rose from their places and slung their AK-47 guns, and duffle bags containing their meager belongings onto their shoulders. Then the six of them slithered through the trees towards the south, planning to bye-pass Pahalgam and enter the main Kashmir valley. It had been a long trek for them through Doda and Kishtawar, after crossing the border north of Jammu, but now they were nearer their goal—and their destiny.

For Gul Bux and his companions it had been a long journey indeed, over the past year and a half. They had fled from Afghanistan, constantly hounded by the foreign forces. They had been told that the country to the south would provide a safe haven, and so they trudged through high mountain passes and entered the mountainous north-west Pakistan. The tribal population there was not all that welcoming towards them, but their contact with the army was a revelation of hospitality. Their Taliban credentials proved to be a boon and they found themselves moved southwards and eastwards till they arrived at camps where they met many others from their own region and with their own ideology. There was also a sprinkling of others from countries more to the west, but with similar way of thinking as theirs: an ingrained motivation to help in the spread of the true Islamic tenets as they were led to believe, so that their misled liberal brethren could be brought back into the fold of the true path. But they all still lacked direction as to how to achieve their aims—adrift as they were from their own countries and their immediate erstwhile objectives.

As they settled slowly into their new unsettled environment, they were gradually shepherded into this new direction. The contacts with the Pakistan army officers were, initially, a friendly interaction meant to build a bridge of common understanding—and, at the same time, to establish the fact that they were now under a strict chain of command that superseded their religious ideology without disturbing its basic tenets. There were times when they chaffed at this new discipline that seemed to enslave them. In their own country they had been used to a less strict regimen: a tribal structure where the chief was sort of a father figure—stern yet kindly. Here the military had a veneer of kindliness, with an intolerant hard core that suffered no disobedience or opposition. They realized that their independence here was circumscribed by the army structure, which imprisoned them within the limits of their camp. There were no fences, but the presence all around them was palpable—even ominous.

As the weeks passed, however, they became more accustomed to their new circumstances and environment; the new discipline started having a more recognizable structure. They were no longer foot-loose tribals with broad objectives of religious intolerance, imposing their whimsical rules on the streets; nor were they loosely assembled groups of armed militia fighting a determined foreign force that never totally understood their environment or culture. Here they were not only being taught a discipline, but also a divisiveness that would help them in a different type of war: a war where the objective was not of overpowering and defeating an opposing force physically, but in instilling a fear that could seep into the psyche of a people—a nation.

Their life was now governed by three forces: the army officers who honed their fighting skills, both in weapons and in physical stamina; the priests who reinforced their extreme religious beliefs and infused the rabid element of sacrificing their lives for their religion and cause; and an unknown cadre of officers who briefed them on the physical and psychological aspect of the new theatre of war they would be required to engage in, in the coming months—once the time was ripe and when they were assumed to be totally attuned to the challenges their battles would require. As part of this indoctrination they were offered an attractive option: a paradise here on earth, or the paradise beyond, that the mullahs had offered.

They were told about this land beyond the mountains that was called the paradise on earth because of its beauty and serenity. They were informed about the mild mannered people that dwelt there in peaceful harmony, unconcerned with their religious differences and customs. They learnt about their Muslim brethren in that land who mingled freely with the infidels, and whose women did not cover their faces and bodies with the black shrouds dictated by their religion. But most shocking of all, this land had been usurped by a nation of infidels, even though a majority of its people were Muslim; all because they had for generations acquiesced to being ruled by Hindu kings.

But now this had to change; was already changing. Over the past two decades people like themselves, the extremists, had been sent across the mountains to teach these mild-mannered people the right path—and for those who refused to learn, a quick death was the lesson to deprive them of their paradise. Had it not been for the infidel army that enforced rule over the land, the battle would have been won long ago. So the battle for them was now on two fronts: to fight this army, and to fight this invidious acceptance of the people to live in harmony with the infidels. This was jihad on two fronts—the overt and the covert; hence, they were told, the training and teaching they had been given over the past months. The time was coming soon, when they would have to cross the mountains in small groups and establish contact with those who had gone before, and those who had already accepted their role as interlocutors for helping in correcting the wrongs of the past.

Thus it was that Gul Bux and his companions found themselves trudging through the mountains, heading for the designated destination to start the final battle. A day earlier they had contacted the bakkarwals in the valley below, to seek guidance on the direction they should take to proceed further. And while leaving the meadow they had picked up one of the lambs that had strayed to the periphery of the meadow. 'Tonight we will have a succulent feast', they chuckled amongst themselves, unaware of the baleful gaze of the little girl who sat in the shade of a tree at the edge of the meadow. Once they had crossed into the forest, the bleating lamb tossed on the shoulder of one of the band, the girl got up, and with tearful eyes went to inform her father of the theft.

∞

"A hunting we will go, a hunting we will go; and catch a fox and put him in a box . . ." sang Roshan in a lusty voice, banishing the peace of the misty morning.

"Don't tell me that you have regressed to your nursery school days," Ravi teased him.

"Anyway, it is more probable that the fox will catch you and put you in his stomach-box, than the other way around," Bashir added.

They all laughed and then continued more quietly down the path. Fairly soon they came across the first of the streams they had been anticipating would cross their path. It was quite shallow, with a rocky bed. It wasn't, however, narrow enough to be crossed with a giant stride or leap, especially with the load on their back. They unhitched their haversacks and looked around for small rocks which they could toss into the middle to build a couple of steps across to bridge the gap. As soon as they had established two seemingly firm central perches for themselves, they picked up their haversacks and prepared themselves to cross the stream by stepping on the stones.

The mist had cleared a lot by now and they could see the smoke rising from the bigger tent of the bakkarwal camp about two hundred yards ahead. But they could also see that they would have to cross another stream—wider and more turbulent—before they reached that camp. On reaching the side of that stream they were relieved to see that part of their task was already achieved: the bakkarwals, most probably, had made an erratic row of stepping stones for crossing the ten foot wide stream. However, as they had gauged from afar, this stream was more turbulent and fast moving. The effect was that the water was already lapping over the stepping stones, flowing over some of them completely. Their dilemma was whether they should try to reinforce the existing effort, or risk getting their shoes and socks wet. The first option could easily cost them around an hour of time; the second one would hardly save them much time, for if they got wet they would have to stop over at the bakkarwal camp to dry out their footwear on their fire. Considering that they had already thought of stopping over for a chat with the bakkarwals, the second option appeared attractive—even though wet shoes do not dry all that easily.

Bashir silently overruled both options by starting on the more pragmatic operation of taking off his shoes and socks; they would cross barefoot over the stones. The others followed suit, removing their shoes and socks and rolling up the bottoms of their jeans. Then they started the crossing in single file, like tight rope walkers, their arms stretched out on either side, holding their shoes and socks.

The water was ice-cold and the first semi-immersion of their bare feet in it sent shock waves up their partly bare legs. When they reached the center of the stream the water was flowing at least a couple of inches over the stones, thus completely swamping their feet and lapping at their ankles. They could not hurry up the speed of their crossing since one slip on the smooth stones would plunge them fully into the current. Gritting their teeth they continued with their agonizing journey. When they finally reached the other side, they collapsed on the damp mossy grass, frantically rubbing their numb feet to revive circulation. Once they had managed to restore some semblance of normality, they quickly put on their socks and shoes and started at a slow trot towards the bakkarwal camp, hoping that they would get some hot drink to thaw out their insides as well.

The bakkarwals had obviously been watching their progress across the meadow and the streams. As soon as the boys came near their camp, they came outside their tents. An older man, who seemed to be their headman or patriarch, waved to them without a word and ushered them into the big tent from which the smoke that they had seen from afar had been coming. He could make out from their shivering bodies and dribbling noses that they were in urgent need of some warm sustenance. He motioned to one of his men to pour out some hot 'nun chai', the typical Kashmiri salted tea, simmering on the stove in a samovar into tin mugs for the boys.

The trio accepted the steaming mugs with gratified grunts and cradled them in their woolen gloves to warm their numb fingers before they touched their lips to the scalding containers. The liquid seemed to pour like hot molten lava down their food pipes, rushing through their bodies to their stomachs. It took some time before they felt warm enough to utter their stuttering thanks. Their gratitude was too deep to be expressed—felt as they did that they had been brought back to life. The patriarch nodded in quiet acknowledgement, then let them finish their brew before he spoke. When they seemed revived enough for coherent communication, he asked them who they were and what they were doing in that area. Ravi, who knew a smattering of Dogri, which was a derivative of his own mother tongue Punjabi, spoke to him. He told the old man that they were students from a school in Srinagar and that their objective was to trek to the base of the Kolhai glacier—and that they planned to reach Lidarwat before that evening.

The patriarch ruminated on this for some time, then in his broken mixture of Dogri and Kashmiri and Urdu spoke to Ravi in a halting voice, "I appreciate your spirit of adventure and the energy of youth that drives you, for we are nomads that travel from place to place. But our lives are driven by our livelihood—to seek ever new pastures for our sheep and goats. We stumbled upon this valley by chance, though we should have traveled through the valley to the south. But, being here, as the benevolent God might have destined us to be, we were perhaps brought here to be the guide to your destiny. Perhaps that benevolent God guided our travels so that we may stand in your path to prevent you from an evil fate. I do not know. But I can see that you are innocent persons and I have to warn you of the perils that you might have to encounter."

He stopped and passed his palms from his forehead down his cheeks, as if washing his face, then continued, "Yesterday we were visited by a band of persons who were not from this region. They asked us for directions, and we gave them as best we could, considering that we ourselves had lost our way. But they were not good people, and after availing of the goodness of our courtesy and hospitality, they stole one of our young lambs, the favourite of my granddaughter's. There was nothing that we could do, for we could notice that they hid long weapons under their cloaks. Who but evil minded persons would do such a deed—seek the courtesy of a tribe and then steal from them? So I can only warn you. Do not proceed further. This is no longer a safe valley. Who knows how many such bands follow them. Wolves travel in packs, but there are always many packs following each other. Beware!"

He stopped, and the boys listened in stunned silence as they absorbed this information. How much of this could they take as truth, how much as an over dramatization of a situation, an incident where they had suffered a minor loss. Could it all be make-belief to misdirect them because of some ulterior motive? But what ulterior motive could the bakkarwal patriarch have in urging them not to continue with their trek?

They finished their warm drinks and thanked their host profusely again; then stepped out into the chill of the morning air. The sun had finally peeped over the mountain to their right, dispersing some of the remaining ground mist. The valley beyond looked enticingly beautiful to them—inviting them to continue their journey. However, as they had stepped out of the warmth of the tent, the chilling warning of the patriarch still hovered over their heads. Should they turn back, or continue on, regardless of the warning?

They walked slowly and quietly through the bakkarwal camp in the direction of Lidarwat, their original destination. All around them were tiny bleating sounds of sheep and goats. There could not have been a more peaceful sight, an almost fairy-like quality to that mist enshrouded valley. No thoughts of violence or evil could even enter such a scene. After they had left the camp behind, they decided to sit on some rocks by the wayside and discuss what their next course of action should be: to go on, or to turn back?

"I think we should carry on," Bashir said, balancing his haversack to take the weight off his back.

"I am not so sure," Ravi said, almost to himself. "Why should the bakkarwals misguide us. Every time the Pakistanis have sent terrorists across the border in the guise of *qabailis*, it has been the bakkarwals or gujjars who have warned the local authorities about their movements. And now, of course, such intrusions are a regular feature in Kashmir since there are so many mountain passes that are difficult to guard. Even though this is not one of the usual routes they use, who knows what new strategy they have evolved."

"Ya, I think we should heed their warning and go back," Roshan put in, looking frightened. "These terrorists are like animals, they will shoot us without asking any questions."

"I am not so sure," Bashir said. "I feel that the old man was just over dramatizing the issue—probably because those people had stolen his granddaughter's favourite lamb. You know how old people are: over protective and over sentimental about their grandchildren. And what if those people took away one small lamb, these gujjars have a whole herd of a few hundred. They must be having animals straying into the mountains all the time— and losing them."

"That's not the point, Bashir," Ravi said. "For one thing, as the old man said, those people had lost their way—so they were obviously not locals. Then what were they doing in this valley? It is too far from the border for any Pakistanis to have strayed into the valley by mistake. And the directions they were seeking were to the villages near Anantnag, and that too by avoiding the Pahalgam valley. Why? We all know that the entire route from Pahalgam to Anantnag is heavily patrolled by security forces. Isn't it strange that these people should want to avoid going by that easier route? Only someone wanting to avoid confrontation with the security forces would want to take the much tougher route over the mountains."

"I agree," said Roshan. "And as the old man said, there could be other such bands following behind them, taking the same route. We should not risk bumping into them and getting bumped off."

"I think you two are being overly sensitive about this terrorist/extremist issue," Bashir said, gazing down the valley. "Just because Kashmiris have now started voicing their desire to shrug off the yoke of Indian domination, everyone feels that they are extremists. Why shouldn't we have the right to run our own lives the way we want to?"

"Because not all Kashmiris want this. We are Kashmiris too—Roshan and I. We are not asking for what you call 'shrugging off the yoke of Indian domination'. We recognize that there has been a lot of suppression and political manipulation, but that is happening all over the country. It is very unfortunate, but I suppose that that is part of the growing up, the maturing of this young country. We have to go through a lot of troughs, before we rise to the crests of the waves."

"Hey! Hey, listen. There you two go again—political debate," Roshan butted in. "I thought that the discussion was on the simple matter of whether we should carry on with our trek, or heed the patriarch's warning and turn back."

Bashir looked at him, seeming reluctant to let go of the argument. Then he said, almost with a trace of bitterness, "I suppose you two can form the majority opinion and veto anything I say."

"I am sorry Bashir," Ravi said contritely, "I did not mean to start a 'yours—mine' debate. But Roshan is right. We have strayed off the path. So let us get back on it."

"Could I suggest a compromise decision?" Roshan said tentatively. "Maybe we should let the next stream decide for us. If the crossing is very difficult, we will turn back."

"But . . ." Ravi started, then decided to let go.

They shrugged their haversacks onto their backs and started across the valley towards Lidarwat. Behind them the gujjars wagged their heads at their foolhardiness; then went into their tents, clucking their tongues in disapproval.

∞

Gul Bux and his band moved through the forest along the mountain slope. They realized that they had taken a wrong route somewhere in the maze of these mountains, but they were not familiar with the area and had to travel going by their instincts, and by the rough directions they had been given when they started off. However, they were not overly concerned, because they still had ample time to reach their destination. They were used to long marches through mountainous country—and this was indeed as beautiful a country as they had been told.

The previous night they had built a spit-roast fire in the shelter of some rocks and roasted their succulent lamb over it. It had been the most satisfying meal they had eaten in many weeks; so, with stomachs full and happy hearts they trudged on, climbing over the mountain top to leave the Lidar valley behind, so that they could avoid Pahalgam and the security forces they had been told heavily patrolled that area. Time enough for that sort of confrontation.

Reaching their contacts in the Kashmir valley was their main objective for now.

∞

As it happened, the evening saw the boys back in the tourist bungalow at Aru—a little bedraggled and enormously disappointed. Gulam Ali was astonished to see them back a day early. He had actually planned to take a short trip to his village for that day, and return the next afternoon with some extra *kadam saag* and rice and *paneer*, to prepare a Kashmiri meal for them when they returned. It was lucky for them that he did not do so, otherwise they would have found the tourist bungalow all locked up and would have had to spend a cold night on the front porch.

"What happened, Sahib. How come you are back so soon?" Gulam Ali asked them. "You were going to come back only tomorrow evening."

"Because of our stupidity in not following your advice," Ravi replied. "We felt that the path going straight through the valley was more beautiful, so we decided to take that. But as you had said, it was more difficult and dangerous. The first two streams were not so bad, and even the third one we managed to cross with a lot of difficulty. But the fourth stream was almost ferocious. We finally decided that we could not take the risk; and since it was too late for us to take the upper path, which you had suggested, we realized that we had no option but to turn back."

"Well, it is good that you did so," Gulam Ali said. "The streams get wider as you go up the valley, especially at this time of the year." He paused, weighing his thoughts before speaking again. "You know, I'm not so sure even the upper path would have been safe for you. After you left this morning, I had thought that I would go to my village up on the mountain for the day. But then I met this woman from Aru village who goes to the forest to collect firewood. She appeared to be very frightened, and warned me not to go to that side. She said that there were strangers camping on the slope of the mountain amongst the trees—and that they seemed to be dangerous. So I turned back and returned to the bungalow. What is the use of taking a risk when there is evil lurking on the mountain. So it is good that you have returned as well."

"Did this woman actually see the men, or just heard about them from someone else?" asked Bashir in a slightly skeptical tone.

"She said that she was picking up firewood in the forest when she saw two men washing their faces by the side of a stream. They seemed to sense her presence and looked up, seeing her through the trees. She did not like the look in their eyes and decided to come back to her hut in Aru. She said that they were dressed almost like the gujjars, and initially she had mistaken them for those. But their faces and eyes were harsh and cruel, unlike the gujjars, who are mild and gentle folk. She also saw that they had kept their long guns by their side as they washed their faces—and that they had reached for the guns as soon as they felt someone watching them. To me it seems that they must be Pashtuns, though we normally never see them in this valley."

"Do you think there is any danger of their coming over here, to this bungalow, during the night?" Roshan asked tremulously.

"I don't think so, Sahib. I heard that they have already gone up the mountain during the day, probably climbing the pass to enter the next valley. God knows where they are headed, or what their plans are. Nothing good I am sure. We are happy to be rid of them," Gulam Ali replied.

"I don't like the sound of all this," Ravi muttered. "Who are these people? What do they want? By all appearances they could be Afghan Taliban, but what were they doing in this valley, and where are they headed?"

They decided to have early dinner and retire to their room for the night, so that they could start back for Pahalgam early the next day.

That night they chatted for a long time in the dark, lying in their sleeping bags on the large double-bed in their room. Just before they finally went off to sleep Ravi said, "You know Bashir, we have been squabbling too much during this trip, and on issues that should not concern us. We have been friends for so many years. Let us continue to nurse the strength of our friendship, rather than dwell on the differences."

Bashir grunted back sleepily. It was difficult to determine in the chill, dark gloominess of the night whether his response was one of agreement, or of dissent.

BOSTON

Now, as he looked out through the window, Ravi thought back with amusement about their truncated trek. They had returned the next day to Pahalgam and checked into a cheap hotel. They did not want to admit to anyone that they had been unsuccessful in reaching the base of Kolhai glacier, so they decided to stay on in Pahalgam for a couple of extra days to fill in the time gap caused by their aborted plan. They utilized that time by sitting by the river, or walking up mountain paths, cooking up stories about how exciting their trekking experience had been. At the back of their minds, however, was the puzzling presence of the band of armed strangers loitering in the mountains above Aru. Ravi had wanted to report the presence of those men to the security forces in Pahalgam, but Bashir dissuaded him. It was all hearsay for them, he insisted; perhaps just cooked up stories concocted by bored mountain folk to lend some excitement and romance to their lives, and to the lives of the boys passing through the valley. I wish I had not listened to Bashir, thought Ravi. Would it have made a difference? Could it have changed the course of events— the course of all that happened subsequently?

Ravi sighed as he thought back on the words of the Gujjar patriarch: perhaps a benevolent God had guided the gujjars' travels, to stand in their path to prevent an evil fate. Perhaps it was the not so benevolent God who had prevented Ravi from conveying the information to the security forces in Pahalgam. But then, who could decide on what God willed—and why? Maybe that was what God's will was: to stand aside and watch the human puppets weave their tapestry. He could not be a Hindu god, or a Muslim god; an Indian god, or a Pakistani god. He could not take sides in the little machinations of puny people. To Him they were all the same. If they created differences amongst themselves it was their problem. If they thought they could convert a paradise into a hell, it was their folly. Perhaps in a decade or two they would come to their senses; for nothing was for ever, and, in any case, every phase was just an altered facet of what had been before. Till then . . .

∞

COLLEGE OR QUIT

Soon after their return from Pahalgam, the School Education Board results were announced. Roshan was amongst the top five students from his school; Ravi a little further down the ladder, though he still managed to squeeze in a first division. Bashir missed his by a few marks, but it sealed his fate anyway; as they say, a miss is as good as a mile. No 'college-follege' for him; he might as well start learning the ropes of the family business. The sooner the better! Shafiq Ahmed was quite firm in his resolve.

Roshan got admission to the Commerce course that he had wanted. Ravi also joined the A. S. College and opted for the B.A course with Economics and History as his main subjects. Since they had classes in the same wing, they met frequently: in the corridors, or in the canteen during free periods. Bashir's absence was troubling to them both, and they went as often as they could to Linking Road in the evenings so that they could cajole him into leaving his shop and join them for a snack at Shakti Sweets nearby.

Bashir told them that his father was still looking out for a suitable opportunity to start a subsidiary shop in India—in Delhi or Chandigarh. Till that opportunity materialized Bashir would be stationed at their shop on Linking Road; but he had also started visiting their suppliers. Later, perhaps, he would take short scouting trips to India to study the market and gauge the potential for their planned future expansion.

To Ravi, Bashir's frequent use of the word 'India', in relationship to the land beyond the Banihal, was irksome; but he decided not to make that an issue for debate with his friend. However, he did express his annoyance to Roshan when they were by themselves later one evening. "Why does Bashir constantly keep referring to the country outside the valley as India, as if Kashmir is not a part of the country?" he asked agitatedly.

"But don't you see," Roshan responded, "Kashmir has always been isolated from the land beyond the mountains. It has always had its own culture and its own traditions that are at variance to those of the outside world. There have been invasions, and conversions to Islam, but the people have continued to live in harmony, untroubled by the winds that blow in the plains. So it is natural to think of Kashmir as one entity and the outside world as another—whether it be India or Pakistan."

"That's true to an extent," Ravi said, kicking some stray pebbles on the path as they strolled along the Bund. "But I get the feeling that there is something more sinister at work here; I do not mean with Bashir in particular, but with the Muslim society here. With every passing year the atmosphere is changing; there is more antagonism in the air. Just a few years back there was more openness in the air—more freedom. Now it appears as if there is something ominous lurking beyond each wall."

"I think you have taken the wrong subjects in college," Roshan ribbed him, slapping him on the back. "You should have taken up English Literature; then you could have written sinister plays of betrayal and intrigue and become the 'Sheikh-Peer' of Kashmir. But seriously, Ravi, you should not get serious over what Bashir says. Even I sometimes inadvertently refer to the land beyond the mountains as India."

"Yeah," Ravi grunted in acknowledgement, "but what I mean is a little bit more than that. Till a few years back one did not feel a sense of alienation from the majority community; it appears almost as if there is a crack developing now, which has the potential to become a chasm. I can sense this in the people working in my father's shop. They are still polite and gentle towards me, but it seems as if they have taken a step back and their behavior now is an act; as if they harbour a resentment, almost as if they were impatiently waiting to bid us adieu—to see us gone forever. It is not a pleasant feeling."

"See what I mean," Roshan said, laughing, "you should still think seriously of changing your subjects at college, so that you can put your natural talents to better use. But I must hurry off now. I promised my father that I would help him sort out some of his shop accounts. After all I must work to earn my daily bread."

And he went off towards Maisuma, leaving Ravi to make his solitary way home across Amira Kadal.

❦

THE SPIDER'S WEB

Colonel Tariq Rehman was on one of his rare leaves of absence from his unit, visiting his father, Rafiq-ul Rehman, at the sprawling bungalow he had built outside Wah after his retirement. It was near enough to Islamabad for him to maintain contact with some of his old colleagues from the army, and yet sufficiently removed for him to seek the isolation that he desired; befitting the image of a broken man who had little to gloat over when he retired as Brigadier after a marred career in the army.

'Kashmir!' he thought with bitterness whenever he sat alone in his garden nursing his glass of whisky. Kashmir was the reason for his ruined career in the Armoured Corps. He had had such a brilliant record in those earlier years and had risen to the rank of Colonel within twelve years of service—an almost meteoric rise for someone so young. His seniors had been quick to recognize his sharp intelligence, his keen acumen for strategic planning, and his undaunted spirit of bravery and leadership. He showed all the signs of rising to higher positions in due course of time.

But then came Kashmir, his first stumbling block; not that he was ever involved in any operation in that sector. Unfortunately, the politicians were obsessed with the idea that they had not been able to gain possession of that jewel for the crown of their country. Their ill-planned, ineffectual effort to annex the valley by force just after independence had totally misfired. Well not totally, since they had managed to claw away some parts of the State before a cease-fire was announced and the UN stepped in. From then onwards it was an endless, frustrating political debate, with no end in sight.

When China attacked India on its North-Eastern flank, and seemed poised to march right into the plains, it was an eye-opener for Pakistan. The weakness of the Indian army had been exposed. That nation of gutless Pandits and shopkeepers could never stand up to the pathans, the warrior race. The Indian army was totally subservient to their wishy-washy, peace mongering political leadership; whereas the political leadership in Pakistan was in the hands of the Generals. This was no match. However, there was still the referee to pay heed to—the UN—which represented the influence and opinion of the world community. Their only chance was to enforce a self-goal: infiltrate as tribals and overthrow the local government in the guise of a local uprising. Brilliant!

It almost seemed as if God was behind them. The Indian Prime Minister, who had guided his nation to independence, had never recovered from the blow of the Chinese betrayal that had buried his slogan of 'Hindi-Chini bhai bhai' in mud. His death brought on a power struggle, and placed on the throne a diminutive, soft-spoken politician as a consensus Prime Minister. No one took him seriously—at least not the Pakistani military establishment, who also held the reigns of political power at that time. The time to strike was now!

Perhaps they were a little hasty with their preparations. Maybe they wanted to utilise the opportunity of the mountain passes opening up with the first summer thaw. Nevertheless they caught the Indians flat-footed, even though the Gujjars, the nomadic shepherds, had cautioned them about the waves of strangers creeping across the border through the passes. They only woke up when the first wave of the infiltrators had reached the outskirts of Srinagar itself. At least the infiltrators were more disciplined this time and did not pause to rape the women en-route to their destination.

It was difficult to gauge what went wrong. The Pakistani planners knew that the Indian army units were largely stationed at the LoC, or Line of Control as the make-shift border between the two countries in the State was called. The second line of defence constituted mainly the State police and a sparse spread of paramilitary forces provided by the Central government to deal with local law and order problems. How could a few thousand infiltrators in the guise of tribesmen be expected to take over the whole valley of Kashmir? The fact probably was that the Pakistani intelligence had grossly miscalculated the amount of local support they would garner in such an operation. As it turned out, the infiltrators who had managed to reach the city had to hole up in a locality on the western periphery of Srinagar. It took just a couple of days to literally smoke them out—and none survived.

However, it soon became apparent that there were many separate units, with independent objectives spread all over the valley. When the Indians belatedly started airlifting additional troops to the valley, some units of infiltrators targeted the lone airport in the valley, trying to make it inoperative. The Pakistani air force tried to lend a hand by sending their fighters and bombers to support the ground units. Neither was successful, and the Indian forces soon started mopping up operations in the valley, flushing out the remaining infiltrators.

The induction of the Pakistani air force into the battle laid bare their true intentions. They were no longer hiding behind tribal cloaks. Being unsuccessful in their efforts in the valley, the Pakistani air force started strafing oil tankers and trucks on the Jammu-Pathankot highway in an effort to cut off supply lines to the valley. The gloves were finally off—it was no longer shadow-boxing. It was open war. The Indians realised that they had to attack along the regular border further south, in order to relieve the pressure that had built up along the LoC. That was where Colonel Rafiq-ul Rehman came into the picture.

Colonel Rehman's battalion was part of the troop build-up that the Pakistani army had been establishing for the past few weeks along the border in Punjab. This was also the sector that provided the road link for supply lines to the State of Jammu & Kashmir; Pathankot being the vital staging point for all such supplies and troop movement. If the Pakistani air force could pulverize that area, their army could move in and cut off that link. Even though they had suffered early reverses along the LoC in J&K, with further supplies and troops not reaching the State the Pakistani army there could recover lost ground.

Colonel Rehman and his colleagues had great pride in their newly acquired American Patton Tanks. With their electronic controls and high fire power and quick maneuverability, they were an unbeatable weapon, and could slice through the Indian army units and reach any destination. 'Delhi, here we come', they thought with mindless bravado.

It was that baseless bravado that led to their ultimate downfall. A large part of their assessment of Indian weakness was based on the Indian army's total rout at the hands of the Chinese in the high mountains of the North-East. That was a totally different terrain and the Indians had never anticipated that the Chinese would attack them, given their oft repeated overtures of friendship and brotherhood. The plains of Punjab were a different proposition and the new young batches of officers who had entered the forces were determined to reverse the ignominy that the army had suffered from the recent debacle at the hand of the Chinese. They led their men from the front and repulsed all Pakistani advances; then gathering courage they counter-attacked, taking the Pakistani infantry by surprise.

The Patton tanks that were brought into play by the Pakistani armoured corps proved totally ineffectual. It became apparent at a very early stage that the personnel manning them had not been able to completely master the sophistry of their machines and weapons. Most abandoned their partially damaged tanks and ran, afraid of an unholy death through incineration. A few managed to race their tanks back to the fast retreating lines.

It was a short war, ending with the Indian army on the outskirts of Lahore, Pakistan's major and ancient city across the border. For a few days the Indians mulled over whether they should overtake the city to crown their victory. But finally they retreated, leaving the Pakistanis to lick their wounds. 'Operation Gibraltar' had ended in a fiasco.

Colonel Rafiq-ul Rehman, one of the few who had escaped the rout, drowned his shame with drink and nursed his hatred for the Indians under the shelter of his cantonment. He was convinced that all their suffering was not because of the lack of bravery of their soldiers, but largely due to the ineffectual inputs provided by the army intelligence mechanism. What were the bastards up to? Why had they not been able to gauge the ground realities in Kashmir? Why were they not able to provide proper inputs on the level of preparedness of the Indian forces? It was not sufficient to be strong yourself, but equally important to know about the strengths and weaknesses of the enemy.

Six years later the dismemberment of Pakistan was the last straw. The formation of Bangladesh out of the erstwhile East Pakistan with the help of the Indian army, which took almost a hundred thousand pure blooded Pakistani soldiers as POWs, was unpardonable!

Rafiq-ul Rehman was Brigadier by then—but of what army? He knew that there could never again be a war between India and Pakistani, for they could never win such a war. But the war, the enmity, the hatred that they harboured in their minds for India, would never die. They had to sharpen new weapons, covert weapons that could sneak in surreptitiously and wound the Indians—again and again and again; inflicting little wounds that would bleed them to weakness without killing them. Kashmir would no longer be the main target; it would just be a pawn in the new game: a pin-prick where they could use the indoctrinated locals as their sacrificial lambs. The whole of India would now be their playground.

His son, Tariq, had just joined the army and Rafiq maneuvered him quietly into the intelligence wing, the ISI, which would be the real brains behind all Pakistani maneuvers against India. He, himself, would remain as the silent manipulator in the background. Rafiq's camouflage of the broken retired army man was perfect. His sharp intelligence and his keen acumen for strategic planning had not dulled with age. They would now come into play on a different front. The embers of vengeance still smoldered within his breast—stoked by the chilled glass of whisky in his hand.

"So, Tariq, how are things going at your end," he asked, twirling the ice cubes in the amber liquid in his crystal glass.

"Going fine, Abba. Over the past two years we have been increasing the number of our terrorist training camps in Azad Kashmir and even further west in Pakistan. We have over thirty such camps now and there is no dearth of recruits. The influx of Taliban has been steady and our infiltrators into the Kashmir valley over the past years have managed to spread discontent in the local people, especially among the youth. As you had assessed, a young man with basic education, but no economic future to look forward to, is fertile ground for rebellion. Our agents have not only been successful in fomenting trouble in the valley, but have also established chains of facilitators who help in guiding these youth over the LoC through the mountain passes to our camps for training. In fact the traffic on this count has been so heavy of late that we have been hard pressed to deal with it."

"But I suggested a solution to you on that count when we talked last," Rafiq interrupted in irritation.

"True, Abba," Tariq said soothingly. "And that is exactly what we are doing. We have established separate training camps for these boys, nearer the LoC. Here we give them some basic training in combat and handling of arms. After two-three months of training we give them fancy titles like commandant or captain and send them back over the passes with some of our old AK-47s and automatic pistols. Even if they are killed in firing along the LoC, they will at least divert the attention of the Indian army while our true blood jihadists sneak in through other routes.

"Good, good," Rafiq said, pouring himself another shot of scotch. "And it is good that you have established separate camps for these boys; if the pathans were to be let loose anywhere near these nubile lads, they would bugger them out of shape—incapacitated for crossing any mountain passes, let alone fighting the Indian forces."

They both laughed uproariously at what was commonly ascribed to be the usual proclivity of the pathans. Then Rafiq asked in a more serious tone, "But what about the situation in the valley? Have we managed to establish an adequate spy network to feed us with information about what the local people feel—how much local help we can hope for this time in our effort to liberate the valley from the Indian yoke?"

"That is one aspect where we have had very good help from the Indian politicians in Delhi," Tariq replied, chuckling with amusement as he leant back in his cane chair. "They are so terrified of the possibility of losing Kashmir that they keep on stumbling over their dhotis in their efforts to keep control. In the last State elections there was such large-scale rigging that it was the last straw for even those Kashmiris who are content with a status quo in the State. The fact is that we are heading for a very interesting scenario. In their efforts at appeasement of the public they have drastically reduced army presence in civilian areas, the responsibility for peacekeeping now being transferred entirely to the local police and the central paramilitary force. The effect is that the fear that the locals had is considerably reduced and they are more willing to openly voice their opposition to the local government or Indian agencies. What is of even more consequence for us is that the overall presence of the Indian army in the valley is actually reduced and restricted to the border areas, or to the cantonment in Srinagar. This could be the ideal opportunity for Pakistan to launch an attack if they wanted to."

"What stupidity is this!" Rafiq-ul Rehman retorted, rising up angrily from his chair. "Haven't I told you many times that that can never be! We have to be circumspect, and surreptitious and cunning. I have told you that Kashmir is no longer a primary issue for us. Let the buggers fight for their own rights. Our role is to ignite the fires and then warm our hands on the ensuing conflagrations from afar."

"Peace father, peace," Tariq said. "I agree with you totally. What I meant to convey was that the atmosphere in the valley has turned very much in our favour. It is conducive to whatever action we might chose to take. Our infiltrators into the valley over the past years have already firmly established themselves in the villages and outlying towns. The local people fear them as much as they do the Indian army and the local police and paramilitary force. For them it is a matter of choice of death by whose sword. With a sizeable section swayed by the slogan of 'azaadi', the favour will tilt towards the terrorists supporting that slogan.

"My plan is to empty out most of our training camps over the next couple of months before the passes close, pushing as many of our hard-core terrorists and raw recruits across the LoC as we can. The former will provide the much needed support for a locally orchestrated uprising, and the latter will provide sufficient diversion for facilitating the crossing of the former. In a few months from now, when the passes have closed and the Indian forces have been lulled into a sense of relative security, we should be able to see our dream of a full-fledged local uprising come true."

"Good," Rafiq said, "we have to keep the fires in Kashmir burning as a foreign policy ploy to keep the dispute between our two countries alive. This also helps to keep the development aid flowing from the Americans— which we can then use to surreptitiously support various terrorist/fundamentalist organizations we are funding in India. But to come back to what you were saying, I can add an element or two to your plan, which will support it and make its success more feasible.

"Last time you told me that you have started the process of creating division amongst the two main communities in the valley. Reinforce this and accelerate these efforts. You see the Kashmiri Pandits hold a large proportion of the administrative jobs within the government machinery as well as the business community. This needs to be highlighted among the Muslims in order to create jealousy and antagonism. Tell them that this is the legacy of the erstwhile Maharaja, and if the Muslims have to claim their legitimate share as the majority community, the Pandits have to go. Fan these fires to the extent that the traditional brotherhood that has existed between the two communities in the valley is broken, and the Pandits are forced to leave. In the rural areas this can be easily achieved by instructing your terrorist cells to start focusing on attacking the Pandits and other minority communities, who have little protection from the security forces in those regions. In the urban areas you will have to create the element of fear and insecurity by instigating threats to the communities through the volatile Muslim youth.

"Once you have managed to start this exodus of the Pandits and other minority communities from the valley, I will initiate the next move . . ."

They talked long into the night, discussing details, till they decided to hit the sack.

CLOUDS ON THE HORIZON . . .

Ramdev Chandra had some unexpected visitors at his house in Wazir Bagh. It was late evening and Ramdev had just reached home after overseeing his shop being closed and shuttered. He had hoped for a quiet evening going through the accounts ledger he had brought home with him, and then a peaceful dinner with his wife, Savitri, and their children. Ravi had just joined college and seemed to be adjusting well to his new routine. Savita was a lively, sprightly girl still in the tenth standard at the Convent School. All seemed to be going well with Ramdev and his family. He was, however, a little troubled by the rumours he had been hearing of late—rumours of unsettled conditions in some of the outlying villages to the west. A lot of villagers came to their godown behind the shop to purchase various hardware materials for repairing their houses, and Ramdev invariably engaged them in conversation to find out what was happening outside Srinagar. A number of them had been talking of strangers taking shelter in their villages, sometimes by force. The news was unsettling in the background of the events of the past few years with increased infiltration into the valley from across the border.

Ramdev's servant Gurbax Singh came to his bedroom to inform him of the visitors. "Seat them in the drawing room on the ground floor and let them know that I will be down soon," Ramdev told him. "And Gurbax," he added, "tell Deepo to take down the tea tray with some biscuits and *bakkarkhanis* for the guests."

He looked out of the windows lining the front of his room while he shrugged on his Nehru jacket and adjusted his shirt collar. The snow-covered peaks of the Pir Panjal mountain range in the distance were turning pink and orange with the rays of the setting sun. There was a slight chill in the air as darkness crept slowly over the valley. The street outside the house was deserted, except for the occasional cyclist going past, belting out some popular Bollywood song. Ramdev came out of his room and descended the stairs at the end of the corridor, wondering why his visitors had decided to come unannounced at this late hour.

"Ah! Rashid! And Ahad!" he uttered in pleasant surprise as he entered the drawing room. Rashid Ahmed and Ahad Bhat were sons of his very close friends. Rashid had risen to the post of Superintendent of Police in the J.K. Police, and Ahad was a Senior Engineer in the P.W.D. Their families and the Ramdevs had always been very close and visited each other's homes on all festive occasions, or whenever there was a family celebration. "So what brings you here at this hour?" Ramdev continued, patting the boys affectionately on their shoulders. "Not that you are not welcome at any time of the day or night, for this is your home. How is Ahmed sahib, and Bhat sahib? Well I hope?"

"All well Sir, with your good wishes. We are sorry uncle," Rashid said softly, "but we felt that it would be best that we visit you at the earliest. In fact Ahad and I were discussing whether we should disturb you at this hour, but when Abba heard what we were talking about, he insisted that we go at once. Abba told me to give you his salaams and convey his best wishes."

"Convey my salaam to your Abba as well when you return, son, but sit down now," Ramdev said, gesturing towards the ornately carved walnut wood sofa with its rich upholstery. "Ah! Here comes the tea, and some things for you to munch on," he added as Deepo entered carrying the tea tray.

The drawing room was tastefully furnished. The ornately carved sofa had a matching pair of chairs on either side. Behind the chairs were tall revolving bookshelves filled with leather bound tomes with titles in golden letters running down their spines. The windows behind the sofa covered the entire front wall width, with heavy flower printed curtains that were half drawn to reveal the orange dusk sky in the background. Opposite the sofa the fireplace was bracketed by two large square heavily padded stools upholstered with the same tapestry cloth that covered the sofas. The mantelpiece above the fireplace was festooned with bric-a-bracs, including some delicate Japanese ceramic figurines. A walnut wood backed couch stood against the side wall, with bookshelves behind it. In the center of the room was an octagonal carved walnut wood table covered with white lace cloth. The room radiated a warm opulence that sparkled in the light of the small glass chandelier that hung above the centre table.

Rashid and Ahad looked around the room with quiet appreciation as they sipped their tea. Then, remembering the gravity of their purpose, Rashid looked up at Ramdev, as if seeking permission to speak. Putting his cup onto the saucer on the small side-table near him, he said, "I am afraid, uncle, the purpose of our visit is a bit unsettling, but the long and close association of our families forced us to come to you at this hour."

"Don't worry son," Ramdev spoke gently, trying to put him at ease. "I am quite certain that your mission is motivated by the desire to seek the best for all our futures. So speak without hesitation."

Rashid continued with more assurance. "The fact is that we have been getting intelligence reports about increased terrorist activity in various parts of the valley over the past weeks. There has been an almost constant exchange of fire between the Indian and Pakistani outposts along the LoC. The reason seems to be that Pakistan has been trying to push across an increasing number of infiltrators—and it appears that they have been successful to a large extent, despite massive casualties suffered by them."

"But that is nothing new," Ramdev interrupted. "This has been almost cyclical every year for the past so many years. Every time the mountain passes open, the Pakistanis push terrorists into the valley to create mayhem here; and the tempo of infiltration increases or decreases almost at their whim till the winter snowfall shuts down the passes again."

"That's true uncle," Rashid continued, almost impatiently, "but the difference is that the rate of infiltration is constantly going up, and so has been the success rate of such infiltrations in past weeks. The army seems to be hard-pressed to cope with this high influx. Normally the JKP and the CRP are able to mop up a large number of these infiltrators in encounters when they reach the villages or towns, but we are increasingly finding ourselves inadequately equipped for the task. Unfortunately, the army does not have sufficient reserves in the valley to bolster our efforts, nor do they have the political mandate to do so. Equally unfortunate is the fact that the local politicians and religious leaders continue to play their populist games and the Chief Minister is reluctant to take any action that could be construed to be anti-Kashmiri."

"I can understand what you are saying Rashid," Ramdev said in a puzzled tone, "but what am I supposed to do? Why are you telling me all this? I used to have political connections to the highest level in the past, but that is no longer true."

"No, no, uncle," Rashid said hurriedly. "I was just trying to give you the background for what I am going to say now—for the purpose of our late evening visit. You see, our intelligence network has not been as efficient as it was expected to be, otherwise we would have found out earlier that the level of indoctrination of our youth by pro-Pakistani elements has been inordinately high in recent months. We stumbled upon the fact quite by accident." Rashid stopped and looked across at Ahad sitting on the other side of the sofa.

Ahad shifted uneasily to the edge of his seat and looked plaintively at Ramdev. Then, clearing his throat, he said, "As you know uncle, my son Parvaiz is eight years old. We did not want to put him in a school that was too far away from home, so we admitted him into a school in our locality, thinking we would transfer him to Don Dosco or some other school after he finished the Primary school level and was old enough to commute to that school by himself. Anyway, the point is that this local school has boys from only Muslim families in the neighbourhood and does not have any community integration.

"A few weeks back, I had come back early from one of my local tours and was having tea in our garden. Parvaiz was marching up and down near the flowerbeds at the edge of the garden, and he was raising his fist with arm outstretched to the sky, shouting some sort of slogan. I did not really pay much attention to what he was doing or saying, till some of his words penetrated my conscious mind. I was shocked to hear the slogan he was shouting in his childish innocence—which basically converted to something like 'kafir Pandits go away, never come back to Kashmir again'.

"I was extremely upset and also very puzzled at how this sort of slogan could have entered Parvaiz's mind—especially since we have a couple of Kashmiri Pandit families living close to our house and we are on very cordial terms with them and exchange visits to each other's homes on festive occasions. After a little while I called out to Parvaiz to come and sit with me, and gently asked him what he had been shouting and who had taught him the slogan. He told me proudly that no one had taught him the slogan—he had learnt it all by himself in school. He explained that all the big boys in school would shout such slogans during break-time, marching up and down near the boundary wall of the playground. Very soon the small boys had learnt the slogans and they would march behind the seniors shouting in unison with them, even though they did not understand the meaning of what they were saying.

"I thought about this for a few days, and then decided to go to meet the Principal of the school. The Principal said that he was aware of what was happening, but was helpless in countering this activity. He explained that a few of the senior boys were listening to the lectures given by some of the *maulvis* after regular prayers at the nearby mosque, and transmitting these thoughts and actions to their friends. It was a pity that all this was percolating to the junior boys during school, but there was nothing that he could do, because the *maulvis* who were the root cause of all this had active support from the fundamentalists and terrorists. To intervene in such matters was like putting one's head on the block.

"I came home very depressed from this meeting, not knowing how I could stop this epidemic. That is when I thought of Rashid bhai and went to him with my woes."

Rashid took up the narrative from there, ". . . which is just as well, because I could at least investigate what was happening. I was as upset as Ahad was to hear all this, and got in touch with my friends and colleagues in the intelligence wing. They were taken by surprise at what I told them. They informed me that they had a network of informers in the rural areas and some in the smaller towns. Even in Srinagar, where they were concentrating on monitoring possible infiltration of terrorists. Though they were aware of the incendiary sermons of some of the *maulvis*, it was too sensitive an area for anyone to do anything about. The thought of monitoring the activities of senior students in local schools had never even entered their minds—nor had they ever given thought to how such anti-communal outpourings could spread to all levels and lead to possible widespread tension that could affect harmony in the valley.

"What is even more alarming," Rashid continued, "as we found out during the course of our investigations, is that this has gone beyond the level of mere slogan shouting. The fundamentalists have formulated specific plans of scaling up aggression towards the Kashmiri Pandits till they are forced to relinquish their livelihoods and homes and flee the valley."

"This is serious indeed," Ramdev said, sitting back in his sofa chair, his brow knitted with a worried frown. "Can't the police do anything about this? Surely you, or the CRP, can provide extra protection to the Pandits to prevent them from coming to harm? I am sure the successful infiltrators have managed to poison the minds of these boys through the *maulvis*. All those educated unemployed youth floating around are equally ripe receptacles for any volatile activity to channel their dormant energies into—just like we witnessed in Punjab some years back when the Pakistanis provided fuel to the "aazadi" call there. This is obviously another one of their nefarious strategies to destabilize the condition in the valley."

"I agree with you uncle," Rashid responded, "but as I mentioned earlier, the JKP and the CRP are finding that

they are overwhelmed by this situation. We just don't
have adequate personnel to handle the problem, and the
army is also not in a position to provide support to us
in internal policing, faced as they are with the escalating
infiltration along the LoC."

"So what do we do?" Ramdev asked with a puzzled
expression. "And, if I may ask again, what am I supposed
to do; why are you telling me all this—what is obviously
sensitive, secret information?"

Rashid clasped and unclasped his hands in agitation,
then nervously taking a sip from the cold remnants of
tea lying in the cup at his side said, "You see uncle, the
assessment made by our intelligence wing, from the latest
inputs received by them, indicates that the strategy is not
limited to coercing the Pandits into leaving the valley;
the wider plan seems to be that once the initial target has
been achieved they will be targeting all other non-Muslim
inhabitants—namely the Punjabis and Sikhs; the ultimate
objective being to make Kashmir a totally Muslim State,
which will make their call for "aazadi", or merger with
Pakistan, that much more realistic and plausible.

"In view of the fact that we do not have sufficient
personnel to protect the entire minority community,
we thought of making an "Option B" solution to the
problem—a quick analysis of the localities where these
communities are residing, to see if we could form a sort
of security cordon around them. The Pandits are, of
course, spread all over the valley and even in large parts
of old Srinagar. It would be next to impossible to provide
protection to all of them. However, a large part of the
Punjabis and Sikhs, and even most of the more affluent

Pandits, are residing in the relatively newer colonies of Wazir Bagh and Jawahar Nagar and Raj Bagh. But when we got around to do detailed planning, we realized that it would be very difficult to provide blanket security to even this limited area—so widespread and porous as it is. Our advice to residents in these areas is therefore going to be that they move to areas closer to the cantonment, at least for the time being, till we are able to achieve better control over the anticipated situation.

"We have not started this exercise at the moment, since we wanted to avoid unnecessary panic, but we will start approaching the residents in these areas very soon to apprise them of the problem. However, since we are aware of the fact that you have another house in the cantonment area that is infrequently used, we felt that it would be best that we let you know at the earliest, so that you have adequate time to make the move. Needless to say, both Ahad and I will provide whatever assistance you will require, both in terms of manpower and transport, to facilitate your moving there."

Ramdev sat quietly, staring sightlessly at the Kashmiri carpet at his feet. A flurry of thoughts swept through his mind—a kaleidoscope of images and sounds linked to this house. He and his father overseeing the construction of the mansion; for that is what it ultimately turned out to be by the time they had finished with it. The family finally moving in, with all his sisters scuttling excitedly from room to room in this large new house, as if the euphoria of release from their previous relatively cramped quarters in the Maisuma house had given them wings; the excited chatter of so many birthdays and festivals and marriages, resounding in the corridors—till now only he and his wife and children were left, with a multiplicity of nostalgic memories. A rich lifetime lived in this structure that had been home to all of them for more than half a century. Even now, most summers, one or the other of his sisters would come visiting with their children for a few weeks of vacation—and the corridors and stairways would echo again with their excited laughter.

And now! His mind suddenly came back to the present with a thud to the stark reality of the predicament confronting him. These two young men, looking so nervously, so anxiously, at him as he sat there lost in his memories, were like sons to him, and yet, could they fathom the depth of attachment and associations he nursed for this house? Perhaps they could, but felt as helpless as he did under the approaching storm.

The room was quiet for a long time as Rashid and Ahad waited, hardly breathing, for uncle Ramdev to say something. At least it seemed as if a long time had passed, though it was hardly a few minutes. Surprising how time—that formless, substance-less entity—could expand and contract to engulf the mind whimsically: to push back the present so that it could momentarily cocoon the pleasant memories of the past and protect them from gathering clouds. Finally, Ramdev raised his eyes and looked at Rashid.

"How much time will I need?" he asked in an even, emotionless voice.

... AND GLOOM

"I would like to apologise to you Ravi," Roshan said in a serious tone, as they strolled on the flood channel bund near their college. "A few weeks back I had made fun of you for making such a serious issue of Bashir's 'Kashmir-India' utterances. Now I can see that you were right to a large extent in your observations."

"So you now feel that I cannot be the 'Sheikh-Peer' of Kashmir," Ravi retorted with a chuckle. "And what has happened to change your mind so soon? Has Bashir said something to you recently?"

"No, no. This is not about Bashir. I still believe that this common perception in Kashmir of anything outside the valley being another country is based on the long isolation our people have experienced through the ages. I am talking about what you said about the feeling of antagonism, of alienation, that you have been feeling of late. Fortunately we have not experienced it in our college, or in this part of town, but when I go home, to the older part of the city, it descends on me like a heavy fog. I am almost afraid of going home after dark. And it is not my perception alone; my father has now started closing his shop an hour earlier for the same reason, even though it means a serious loss of business for him since a lot of his regular customers come later in the evening."

"Why, what is happening? What are you so frightened of?" Ravi asked him anxiously.

"It started a few weeks back—a little after I had joined college," Roshan continued. After our normal routine of meeting Bashir after college I would visit my father's shop and then start for home. At the head of the lane leading to our house in Habba Kadal, there has always been this group of boys who hang around gossiping. In recent weeks I noticed that they would start giggling amongst themselves whenever I approached and pass snide remarks, obviously meant for me, though not aimed directly at me. I ignored them, thinking that it is not unnatural for boys their age, about fourteen or fifteen years old, to pass funny remarks aimed at passersby: that it was part of their adolescence, their newfound bravado. However, as days passed, I felt that their remarks and their body language were getting increasingly more bold and aggressive, till they started blocking part of the road as I approached, even brushing against me as I went past them. Last week, after I had crossed them, side-stepping their jostling movements, one of them shouted after me, 'Oye Pandit, do your prayers while you have the time, you might not get the opportunity later', and they all burst out laughing. It is very disconcerting; these are the same boys who, till a few months back, used to come to me to plead to me to show them how to spin the cricket ball, or play the cover drive."

"I can understand what you feel Roshan," Ravi said, putting his arm around his shoulders. "This is bad. Why haven't you talked about this to your friends in the locality—the older boys with whom you used to play cricket on Sundays? Maybe they can help curb this behavior?"

Roshan looked forlorn as he said, "That is the other problem. Those boys, who used to be my friends and whom I played with every Sunday, have started avoiding me. Last Sunday I went to our neighbourhood playground thinking I'll play cricket with them. The game was about to start when one of them spotted me coming. Earlier I used to be a welcome member of any team, but this time he shrugged me off saying, 'no space for you Pandit, we have already selected the teams'. I could see that neither team was up to strength—that this was just an undisguised move to exclude me. But what was even more galling was the fact that this chap did not even have the decency to call me by my name, even though he knew me well."

"I wish I knew what to say," Ravi said sadly, "except that I hope that this is a passing phase; that things will improve and return to their former state. However, I get the feeling that we are going downhill; there is some outside force manipulating our lives. I know that this repeated rigging of State elections has caused a crisis of faith among the people, so that they increasingly feel that they are no longer masters of their own destiny, but that is no reason for them to treat us—the non-Muslims—with antagonism. We cannot be held responsible for all the mess, then why are they turning against us? I am confident that this is also part of Pakistani strategy—not unlike what they have done with Muslim youth, in convincing them to cross the LoC for training in arms for fighting for their 'aazadi'. All they are interested in is to create martyrs, for they know that a large number of those who try to come back will be shot when they try to sneak back across the LoC. And that will stoke the fires of discontent among the local population against the army, heighten the trend for fundamentalism and create discord among communities. How else can one explain this newfound antagonism that you are talking about?"

"What you say might be true," Roshan said angrily, "but you are talking in theoretical terms, the psychology behind what is happening—a rationalisation. I am faced with the stark reality, a looming crisis. What do I do? What do we all do? For even my father has not escaped their barbs; as I said even he has started closing his shop early so that he can come home before dark. My mother, my sister—we are all living in a state of apprehension, of fright."

Ravi thought for a moment, then said, "All I can suggest is that you be patient—do not retaliate to their barbs and abuses under any circumstances. I, in the meantime, will approach Rashid Ahmed, who is the Superintendent of Police in JK Police. His father and mine have been close friends for a long time, and our families are very close to each other. I will relate to him what you have told me, and see what he has to say. Rest assured that I will bring some news to you within a few days. Till then, as I said, be patient and do not react to what these hooligans say or do in the intervening period."

SHIFTING SAND

When Ravi reached home later that evening, he saw that a big truck was parked just inside the main gate, almost blocking the entrance. He was puzzled to see it there and sidled his way in through the small gap between the truck and the gate on one side. What was happening? Why was the truck there at this time of the evening? Why was it there at all? Had his father ordered some more furniture?

Once he had reached the rear end of the truck he realized that he had been totally wrong. Furniture was being loaded on to the truck, not unloaded from it. But why? Then he realised that the stuff being loaded was from their drawing room. He back-tracked the string of labourers carrying out the things and reached the drawing room and peeped in. In the midst of the bare walls and flooring hung the crystal chandelier, forlorn at the loss of all its companions—glimmering palely in its loneliness. Ravi felt a lump constricting his throat at this desolate scene, then ran swiftly up the wide staircase to the first floor. His parent's bedroom door was slightly ajar and he could hear a faint murmur of voices from inside. He burst in, breathless, with only a cursory semblance of a knock, "Papaji, what is happening . . . ?"

"Come in Ravi, come in," his father said, leaning back in his armchair near the front windows. "I can imagine the reason for your breathless stampede up the stairs. I suppose I should have talked to you about my plans earlier. But it was all a bit sudden. You see, I've decided that we should all shift to our house in Shivpura for a few months."

"But why so suddenly?" Ravi interrupted. "And why all of us? My college is just down the road from here, from Shivpura it will be a long commute for me every morning and evening. Couldn't I just stay here by myself? And why are we moving all the furniture from here—don't we have enough in the Shivpura house?"

"Ravi, just because I was polite to you just now does not mean that you start questioning my decisions," Ramdev said sternly. "For one thing, when I decide that the family will move, then the whole family will move! We are just four of us anyway, and I don't want that we should be separated. In any case I cannot afford to leave one servant here just to look after you. We will all have our own rooms there, just as we have here, so there is no inconvenience to anyone on that count. As far as commuting is concerned, the car goes to drop Savita to her school from here every morning, which it will do from there as well. You will just have to leave for your college along with her—or if that is too early, you can come with me every morning when I come to the shop. Otherwise you can use the public transport, and I will increase your allowance accordingly. As far as moving the furniture is concerned, we are moving only the drawing room furniture. I wanted to have the room completely renovated since I noticed that there was a lot of dampness on the walls, and I did not want to leave all the stuff out here while the workers are around—you know how they mishandle stuff. So there! I hope that answers all your questions."

Ravi stood still. He noticed that his mother had a mournful expression on her face as she sat on the edge of the bed. She was obviously as upset by what was happening as he was. Not wanting to upset her, or aggravate the situation further, he murmured quietly, "I am sorry Papaji. It was just such a sudden shock that I didn't realise that I was being rude. Please let me know if I can help in any way." And he left the room, unhappily shaking his head with annoyance as he slowly climbed the staircase to his room on the second floor.

"Why didn't you tell him the truth?" Savitri asked her husband as she heard Ravi going up the stairs. "I am sure that he would have understood what's happening; he is grown up enough."

"It is not that Savitri," Ramdev said in a low, contemplative tone. "I know that he is grown up, but, at the same time, emotionally he is still a child. What Rashid told me was in strict confidence, for our family's welfare. I must honour that confidence. Ravi has a number of friends in college who are Pandits: that Roshan Bhan, for example, who is his best friend. Ravi would feel obliged to share the information with him, to protect him and his family from harm, and then the news would spread and create panic. That is exactly what Rashid and the authorities are trying to prevent. I feel bad about not being able to share the knowledge that I have with him, but I have no alternative. And you must be cautious as well in what you say to the children or to anyone else. We must maintain the pretence to all that we are shifting temporarily in order to get some renovations done to the house. That is why I have gone to the extent of moving some of the furniture to the other house. Of course it is equally true that most of that furniture and the books are part of the legacy left behind by my father—things that he so fondly collected or got made. They have a sentimental value for me and I cannot stand the thought of losing them in case something was to happen to this house. There are some things in life that cannot be brought back with money. I would rather hold them close to me as long as I can.

"I will be leaving our old watchman, Gulla, to look after this house while we are away. I hope we can come back again soon. And I hope that Rashid can arrange some occasional patrolling by his policemen in this area as a precaution to avoid any mishaps. Let us just hope and pray that the authorities will be able to prevent the situation from getting out of control."

The next few days were hectic for all of the family. Though the Shivpura house was fully furnished, it had to be thoroughly cleaned before they could even start moving in. Also, Savitri had to ensure that all provisions were bought and stocked for making the new household operative. Then everyone had to pack all their personal belongings for moving to the other house. Though Savita continued to go to her school, and Ramdev went to his shop every day, Ravi and his mother had to bear the burden of overseeing all the practical details of the shifting exercise—with the effect that Ravi was not able to go to college for a week.

Roshan wondered what had happened to his friend; once when he went past Ravi's house in Wazir Bagh, he could see a lot of cardboard cartons and suitcases being loaded onto a tempo goods carrier. But there was no sign of Ravi. Had he forgotten about his promise of talking to Rashid Ahmed? That could not be, for Ravi was too sincere a friend. Then what? Ravi had told him to be patient—but the situation was getting worse day by day. The Bhan family seemed to be standing at the edge of a precipice.

∞

Roshan was walking down the road towards his house when he heard a loud rumble of approaching trucks. Far down the road some police trucks emerged out of a cloud of dust. In the large manhole type opening on top of the cab of the leading truck stood a helmeted policeman with a stengun in his hands. Suddenly, from behind Roshan, there materialised a crowd of young boys wearing faded jeans and *phirans*. As the convoy of trucks drew near, the boys started lobbing big stones at the trucks. The stones clattered loudly as they hit the steel sides of the trucks. The policeman on the cab of the truck opened fire with his stengun. The noise of the crackling gun fire and the clatter of stones against the trucks grew louder by the minute. Roshan felt that he was falling into a ditch and he clamped his hands to his ears in terror.

He woke up with a start—disoriented. Where was he? "Wake up sleepy heads, Gulam Ali is here with the tea," he mumbled in his fuddled semi-wakefulness. Then he felt a hand shaking his shoulder firmly, and a voice whispering hoarsely in his ear, "Wake up Roshan. They are attacking the house."

Roshan sat up in his bed with a start. His father was standing by the side of the bed. The room was dark, with just a faint glow of night light showing beyond the rectangular window frame on his right. He could now clearly hear the clattering of stones on the corrugated tin sheets of the roof above him, and their rumbling as they rolled down the slope of the roof to fall to the ground with a thud. Roshan crept to the window and peered out from one side. It was semi-dark outside, with just a dim ghostly star-lit sky washing over the little apron of a garden in front of the house and the dark grey lane beyond their boundary wall. He could see a few dark shapes scurrying about in the lane, and the abrupt jerk of robe-clad arms as they lobbed their missiles towards the house.

Roshan sensed his father standing behind him, breathing heavily. He was pressing down heavily with his hands on Roshan's shoulder, partly transmitting his own fear, partly in an effort to restrain Roshan from doing anything rash. He soon realised that whoever was throwing the stones was deliberately targeting the roof, rather than the glass windows at the front of the house. The idea seemed to be to create a racket and cause panic— or maybe convey a warning. Was it those boys who stood at the head of the lane every evening and passed snide remarks at him as he went past them? The night was still young enough for them to be out for a night stroll.

In his anger Roshan forgot all about Ravi's advice of patience and caution and shouted, "Oye, what do you think you are doing, disturbing our sleep. Go away before we call the police."

There was a deadly silence for a moment, then a boyish voice shouted back, "The police cannot protect you Pandit, but we can. Or rather we can protect your house and your sister. The rest of you go away. We will take good care of your sister when you are gone." Then there was derisive laughter and the shadows in the lane disappeared.

Roshan was shaking with rage now, but his father dragged him away from the window, whispering harshly, "Stop it! You know you cannot pick a fight with those hooligans; shut up and keep quiet!"

Roshan slumped onto his bed, bitter and frustrated. His father was right—there was nothing he could do. He had to be patient. Ravi had been right. But for how long? And where was Ravi in any case? He had promised to talk to the person in the JK Police, but that was days back. Now things seemed to be getting out of hand, when these boys were even threatening them in their own house.

<hr />

Ramdev came back from his shop that evening a troubled man. It was over a week since Rashid and Bhat had visited him. Ravi and Savitri had handled the move to the Shivpura house with the help of a few employees that had been spared from the shop and the godown. The gardener at the Shivpura house had managed to muster a few of his acquaintances to come and help out with the cleaning of the house, so that the family was able to start moving in with all their personal belongings within four days; and Gurbax Singh was able to get the kitchen going even before they had fully moved in. So everything had worked out with efficient precision and they were all now settled in.

Ramdev's unease, his apprehension, his sense of discomfort was, therefore, not on that account, nor anything to do with his shop. Well, it was obliquely to do with his business. As per his normal practice he had visited his godown that day to have a chat with the farmers coming for supplies. Surprisingly, business was not as brisk as it should have been during this peak season, and those who were there wore grim expressions. Their responses to Ramdev's queries were taciturn and glum. Since he was familiar with some of them, he managed to ferret out some information from them.

Things were not so good in their villages, they told him. There were strangers holed up in their villages; cruel-faced, vicious looking pathans who threatened them into silence and submission. They had installed their own *maulvis* in the mosques, who used the loudspeakers to spew out the tenets of jihad—death to the infidels, the non-believers, they urged in the name of Islam. There had been killings—of Kashmiri Pandits and Sikhs who lived in those villages. A large number of the remaining had abandoned their homes and fled to save their lives. These were their brethren: their neighbours and friends who had been a part of their lives for decades—for generations.

But what could they, the Muslim villagers, do? They had tried to plead for them, provide them with protection and shelter for some time. The pathans branded the sympathisers as traitors and slaughtered them along with the people they sheltered. All the Pandits and Sikhs had now been slaughtered, or had fled. They, the Muslim villagers, now lived in dread of their new masters and the local collaborators who provided them with shelter. They had come to Srinagar to buy their necessities, but were never sure whether anyone was watching over their shoulders in case they revealed their situation to anyone here—which could lead to repercussions on their families back home. They whispered all this to Ramdev, at the same time begging him not to say anything to anyone. They were relieved to unburden their secrets to him, but, at the same time . . .

Ramdev did not have to reveal anything to anyone; the information he had gathered corresponded to and confirmed what Rashid had already told him. It also confirmed what Rashid had said—that they did not have sufficient security forces to cover all the troubled areas, and that was why the terrorists had a free run in the outlying villages. What was disconcerting was that the juggernaut of conspiracy was already rolling—the sparks of the fire were already lit. How much longer would it take for the conflagration to reach Srinagar?

For the first time Ramdev started having doubts about his own conduct, his own motives. Had he been overly discrete in his actions over the past week? It was true that Rashid had spoken to him in confidence, but if there were lives at stake, should he not have warned at least some of his Pandit and Punjabi friends? Should he not have shared his information with his own son—so that Ravi could have at least warned and protected his closest friend, Roshan? These doubts now gnawed at his conscience. What had earlier been just a conjecture, a possibility on the far horizon, had suddenly been transformed into a stark reality.

That evening, sitting at the dining table, be broached the subject cautiously. "Bad news from the villages," he mumbled as he chewed his food, not looking up from his plate.

Savitri and Ravi looked at each other in silent enquiry, then at him, waiting for him to say something more. They had noticed his preoccupied air when he had returned from work. Instead of sitting in his study and going through his ledgers or reading a book as he normally did, he had been pacing up and down on the large lawn in front of the house, even after darkness had fallen. They had wondered what was wrong, what was troubling him. It seemed that he had now decided to unburden his mind to them. They waited tensely, slowly chewing their food, as if afraid that even the sound of their chewing might disturb him. On the other end of the table Savita sat unconcernedly, humming quietly to herself, lost in her own thoughts as she picked at her rice and curry—unaware of the tension.

"I have been talking to the villagers who come to buy stuff from our shop at this time of the year," Ramdev continued, still looking down at the food on his plate between bites. The others waited, not wanting to disturb his train of thought with unnecessary questions.

"The news is not good," Ramdev continued, looking up now, first at Savitri, then at Ravi, his brow knitted in a worried frown. "The villagers I spoke to were frightened, subdued by what was happening there. According to them a large number of infiltrators, terrorists from across the border, had firmly established themselves in their villages with the help of local sympathisers. But what is even more worrying is the fact that they are no longer content with launching attacks on the security forces that try to flush them out, their targets are now the minority community living in those villages: the Kashmiri Pandits and the Sikhs and other Punjabis. A lot of killings have already taken place. They are trying to flush out all the minorities; and any of the local Muslims who try to prevent these killings, or to give them shelter, are equally viciously slaughtered. In most villages all the people from the minority communities have fled, leaving behind burnt houses and shops. Unfortunately the number of local sympathisers, the 'azaadi' brigade, are increasing, effectively subduing the voices of those who are against these atrocities. According to what the villagers have heard, the new strategy seems to be to cleanse the valley of all non-Muslims, so that the voice of those who want 'azaadi', or merger with Pakistan, becomes more coherent and their demands more acceptable to the world community."

"So what Roshan had said was not far from the truth," Ravi muttered thoughtfully, half to himself.

"What did Roshan say?" Ramdev asked apprehensively.

"That the boys in his neighbourhood, in Habba Kadal, were getting increasingly aggressive towards him and his father every time they passed—taunting them and making snide comments." Ravi suddenly looked up startled and said guiltily, "Oh God! With all this shifting work I had clean forgotten that I had promised him that I would talk to Rashid Ahmed about what he had told me. I haven't even met Roshan for over a week. What must he be thinking? What an ungrateful friend I have been."

Ramdev looked at Savitri, as if seeking support, a pained expression on his face. Then turning to Ravi he said guiltily, "Unfortunately Rashid will not be able to help."

"But why?" Ravi asked incredulously. "He is Superintendent Police in the JKP; their task is to provide protection to all citizens. Is it not part of his duties to oppose such blatant acts that are obviously aimed at threatening a family from the Pandit community—a family that has lived there for a few generations? Who are more a part of this valley than even our family is?"

When Ramdev spoke his voice was quiet, almost an undertone, "Ravi, this is the second time this week that I have had to apologise to you. Today, I have no desire to counter whatever you might say or do, for I feel truly guilty for not having taken you into confidence of what I had learnt at that time." Ramdev paused, and then in an even, emotion filled voice he recounted to Ravi the events from that evening visit of Rashid and Bhat; what they had related to him and what they had suggested—which had led to his hurried decision to move out of Wazir Bagh.

The rest of the meal was left to cool on their plates. What they had already eaten felt like cold stones in their stomachs. So, they had fled to safety from the impending storm, leaving their friends to fend for themselves, not even giving them the benefit of a warning? That's what agonised Ravi, even though he himself had not been privy to the information. Ramdev could fathom his agony— and, for once, shared his son's acute feeling of guilt.

When Gurbax Singh came to clear the table along with Deepo a little later, he saw the half eaten food on the plates and anxiously asked his mistress, "Why Bibiji, was the food not well prepared? Did I put too much salt, or chilies?"

Savitri had no answer; she felt within her heart that they had denied the salt that they had shared with their friends. She quietly got up and went to her room.

∞

The next morning Ravi got up early and left in the car which was going to drop Savita to her school. He had spent a restless night, and was determined to go to college early so that he could meet Roshan before his classes started. Since it was still very early by the time they had reached Savita's school, he told the driver to go back home, and he would walk the rest of the way to college.

The morning was clear and crisp and he felt invigorated as he walked along the Bund, watching the Jhelum flow sluggishly past the shabby houseboats down below. Far on the horizon to his right, a long way beyond the bend that took the river past Amira Kadal, he could see a vague sort of dispersed grey cloud against the bright blue sky all around. Could it be the tannery spewing early morning pollution through its tall chimney? But they normally did not fire their furnaces that early in the morning. Maybe a fire somewhere? That was not uncommon with all the wooden structures standing cheek by jowl in the old city.

He brushed aside his speculations about the grey cloud and started thinking of his impending meeting with Roshan. What would he say to him? What *could* he say to him about his callous behavior? There was no justification that he could offer—especially after the facts that had been revealed to him last night. That would be equivalent to tightening the moral noose further around his neck. Perhaps he would tell Roshan that he had finally met Rashid after trying for a number of days—and Rashid had told Ravi about the gravity of the situation the security forces were facing in the valley? He could tell Roshan that it would be advisable if their family moved out from the Habba Kadal area for a few weeks, till things settled down. Then he realized that Roshan would have learnt by now that they had moved out of their Wazir Bagh house over a week back, and would immediately connect Ravi's advice to him now as a belated warning of what they themselves had heeded much earlier. His lie would be caught out, but no matter—better late than never. He had to go through with this, even if it meant demeaning himself in his friend's estimation.

At Lal Mandi he left the Bund and went down the road that went past their Wazir Bagh house towards his college. Their house looked desolate, with all the windows closed shut and not a soul around. At an impulse Ravi pushed at the gate, but it was locked from inside and his vigorous knocking and banging produced no result. Gulla must have gone out somewhere through the small back door. In any case his stopping there was just a sentimental whim; his main objective was to reach the college early so that he could talk to Roshan—and he hurried on.

At the college there was a trickle of students going in. Some of the early birds were already clustered around in small groups on the lawn inside, enjoying the warmth of the early morning sun with dew glistening at their feet. As Ravi walked along the gravel path towards the main building, someone called out to him from behind. He turned around in anticipation of seeing Roshan—but it was Rafiq, one of his classmates walking towards him.

"Hi Ravi," he said as he reached him and shook his hand. "Where have you been? Haven't seen you for over a week? We were wondering what had happened to you— you haven't been ill have you?"

"No, no," Ravi responded. "Father wanted me to help him out with something, so I had to skip some classes. I hope I haven't missed anything important?"

"Nothing *yaar*," Rafiq replied. "You know how it is with these professors; they read out the same notes they have taught from year to year for decades. You can copy the notes I have taken down and you will have caught up with what you missed over the past week. By the way, had you all gone out of town or something? I noticed while passing your house that there seemed to be no one around, and all the windows were shut."

"No, not out of town," Ravi answered hurriedly, "we have just shifted for a while to our house in Shivpura, because father wanted some repairs done here and some repainting work. He didn't want us to be here while that was being done—what with all the dust flying around and the smell of paint. We should be back here in three-four weeks once all the work is finished."

"I envy you *yaar*. You are lucky to have another house to shift to. We had to bear with all the paint smell last year, when my father had our house repainted."

By then a number Ravi's other classmates had joined them and there were handshakes and greetings all around. Ravi had half his attention focused on the gate, hoping to catch Roshan coming through. He was getting restless now, since it was almost time for the first class to start. Why had Roshan not come so far, he wondered? He was always early in reaching college. Was something wrong? When someone mentioned that it was time for their first class to start, he reluctantly joined them as they walked towards the building. He did not want his friends to wonder why he was skipping class even when he had arrived early in college. His mind, however, was not on what the teacher was saying, and he let the droning lecture float over his head, waiting impatiently for the class to end.

As soon as the bell rang and the teacher gathered his papers and exited through the front door, Ravi bolted out of a side door before anyone could engage him in conversation. He walked briskly towards the wing where Roshan had his classes. He saw a few of Roshan's classmates clustered around a door, waiting for their next class to begin. He barged into the group without greeting or apology and anxiously asked them if they had seen Roshan. They looked at him with mild disdain at his uncouth behavior, then they seemed to decide to humour him. No! one of them told him, they had not seen Roshan around for the last two-three days. Then they turned away from him and continued with their conversation.

Ravi was distraught. What should he do now? He did not know Roshan's residential address, having never gone there. Then he thought of Bashir. Yes, that was it! Since he had not been able to establish contact with Ravi, Roshan would have gone to meet Bashir. After all he was the one they went to meet almost every evening after college. Ravi left college and headed for Linking Road.

∞

FRIENDS AND FOES

Roshan had indeed gone to see Bashir a few days earlier. Not having heard from Ravi for many days, he felt the need to explore other options for assistance. After the stone throwing incident the previous night, he was desperate. Ravi's assurance of help had restored some of his confidence. But now, Ravi was nowhere to be found.

Roshan met Bashir at his shop in the afternoon, at a time he knew he would be relatively free. He asked him if he had seen Ravi in the past few days. Hearing Bashir's reply in the negative, Roshan told him that he needed to talk to him urgently about something serious—could they go to the Bund where they could talk in private? Bashir could see that Roshan was very agitated, almost to the point of tears. He told his assistants that he would be back in about half an hour and they walked across to the little park on the Bund.

They settled down on a concrete bench under the shade of a gigantic chinar tree. There was no one around at that time of the day, except for a couple of labourers stealing a nap on the grass under another tree some distance away. Roshan began his narrative in a low, agony constricted voice. He told Bashir about what had been happening over the last couple of weeks: the mild teasing and threatening that became more aggressive with each passing day, till they had not even spared his family. And now, with last night's incident of stone throwing at their house, and their open threats and lewd innuendos, things seemed to be heading for some sort of climax.

Roshan told him that he had talked about all this to Ravi, who had promised to try and help. But now there was no sign of Ravi—who did not even know of last night's incident—and Bashir was the only other close friend he could approach for help. He looked at Bashir beseechingly, his eyes watering with the helplessness he felt. Bashir looked down thoughtfully at the dry patch of earth at their feet, soaking in all the information that Roshan had relayed to him. He was concerned for the welfare of his friend and his family. Roshan and Ravi and he had been close friends for over ten years, all the way through school, and though Ravi and he had often held divergent views on various issues and quarreled occasionally, Roshan had always been the moderator between them—the balm that soothed any acrimony.

Bashir looked up at Roshan and asked, "Do you think it would help if I came to your locality and talked to these boys?"

"I don't think so Bashir," Roshan said. "I don't think it is just these boys. They would never have the guts to do what they did last night. There is obviously some other more powerful body that is inciting them and providing them with the courage to act so outrageously. I would not want you to be enmeshed in a fight that could have serious repercussions."

Bashir thought again, then placing a sympathetic hand on Roshan's shoulder said, "Then wait. I will talk to my father to see if he knows someone who can help—perhaps someone in that locality. Meet me again tomorrow evening, and let's see if I have some more hopeful news for you."

❧

Later that afternoon, when his father came to the shop after his lunch and siesta at home, Bashir followed him to his little cubicle of a private office. After shutting the glass paneled door, Bashir told him about his conversation with his friend earlier in the afternoon. Shafiq Ahmed listened quietly as his son repeated all that Roshan had narrated to him. The *pilau rice* that Sameena had served to him for lunch had been particularly good and he had overeaten. He could still savour the rich fragrance of its saffron. Though his after lunch nap had helped to partly digest the meal, it still sat heavy in his stomach. He had returned to the shop in a mellow mood, but Bashir's narrative was now making his stomach rumble. He burped loudly, then said, "Why do you want to get involved in this Pandit boy's problems? Why can't he just go to the police for help? That is what they are there for. What can we do?"

"Abba, they have been to the police, especially after last night's incidence. But the police just put them off saying that this was just boys having fun. 'Has anyone attacked you physically, or damaged your property? On what basis can we take action?' And they sent them off without even registering a complaint."

"And that is true—what the police said," Shafiq Ahmed said settling deeper in his chair. "They can't file complaints on the basis of what young boys have tauntingly said. And what can I do? If I go to someone with the same story, I am liable to get the same response as well."

"But Abba, isn't there something we can do? Roshan and Ravi and I have been very close friends for such a long time; all the way through school and even now. They are almost like my brothers. Perhaps you know someone in Habba Kadal area who can help?"

"Oh, so you are no longer content with having two grown up sisters, you now want two brothers as well," Shafiq said chuckling humorously after another loud saffron fragrant burp. "But you have been a good son, and have learnt our business very fast and taken a lot of burden off me, so I will see what I can do to unburden your mind over this issue. I do not know anyone in that part of the city, but I will see if I can think of someone who might be able to help."

Shafiq Ahmed did not tell his son, but he had thought of someone whom he could approach; someone whom he had been close to some twenty years back, but with whom he now maintained a distance, except for occasional semi-accidental contacts. When they bumped into each other at some official function or the other, they were as affectionate to each other as they had been in earlier days, but Shafiq was a little cautious now because he did not want to get involved in the divisive politics of the valley. The fact was that his erstwhile friend, Abdul Gani Shah, was now head of the Freedom and Self-rule Party, the FSP, which was anti-government and anti-India and had therefore gained a lot of popularity over the past decade, especially with the radical and extremist elements and the youth. With a dint of probing and prodding Shafiq Ahmed managed to get Abdul Gani's telephone number and get a message through requesting a meeting. Within an hour he got a call saying that 'Jenaab Abdul Gani Shah Sahib' would be pleased to see him at his residence in Fateh Kadal at 7 p.m. that evening. The details of the residence were conveyed to him by the caller. Shafiq was pleasantly surprised—he had not expected such a prompt response, and such an early meeting. After all 'Jenaab Abdul Gani Shah Sahib' was an important man.

∞

Shafiq Ahmed left his shop soon after 5 p.m. He had not told Bashir anything about his plans, because he did not want to raise his hopes unnecessarily. Sameena was surprised to see him back so early and quickly went to prepare some *kavah*, the Kashmiri spiced green tea, and laid out some bakkarkhanis to go along with it. Their teenage daughters, Salima and Sabah, were back from school and could be heard chattering loudly in their room at the back of the house.

Shafiq explained to his wife that he had to go for an important meeting and asked her to take out his formal *pathani salwar* and long shirt and *jooties*, which he normally wore for parties, while he went to wash up. Half an hour later he came out of his room dressed in his crisp formal clothes, dabbing a little *ittar* behind each ear. Sameena looked at him appreciatively, then asked him with a coquettish smile, "So who is this 'special' person that 'jenaab' is going to meet this evening, dressed up in such finery?"

Shafiq responded with equal flippancy, "Why should I tell you? Some things are better concealed from the wife." They both burst out laughing. Then Shafiq said in a serious tone, "I have to go and meet my old friend Abdul Gani Shah. I had requested a meeting and he sent back a message saying that I should come to his house at 7 p.m. today. He is an important person, so I have to dress up for the occasion, even though it is just a private meeting."

"Abdul Gani Shah? That leader of the FSP?" Sameena asked, a bit startled. "I hope everything is alright? You have not got into any trouble?"

"No, no. I have no problems," Shafiq said quickly, not wanting to go into any details. "Someone wanted a favour, and knowing that we had once been close friends, asked if I could intercede on his behalf. I could not refuse." He got up and went towards the front door. Then turning back he said, "I will probably be a little late for dinner since I have to go all the way to Fateh Kadal, so you and the children don't wait for me."

While getting into the car he told the driver that they had to go to Abdul Gani Shah sahib's residence in Fateh Kadal, giving him the address. The driver gave him a startled look, but did not say anything. Closing the door after Shafiq had settled down in the back seat, he went around and started the car. Giving a long angry blare of the horn, he headed out of the gate.

They reached Abdul Gani Shah's residence at ten minutes to seven. The house stood in the middle of a crowded locality of double-storied wood and stone houses, typical of the architecture of the old city, built almost a century back. Shah's house however had a grey boundary wall eight foot high, covering a length that would have encompassed four of the older structures. The wall was topped by a roll of protective barbed wire fencing running along its entire length and disappearing with it around the corners on both sides. In the center of the wall was a large steel double-paneled gate, with the top of a sentry box jutting over the wall on one side. As Shafiq's car drove up and stopped near the gate, a sentry peeped out through an aperture in the sentry box. A minute later one of the panels of the gate opened a crack and a guard slipped through it and approached the car. Shafiq lowered his window glass and gave his name and told the guard that he had an appointment with Shah sahib at seven that evening. The guard looked closely at him and at the interior of the car, then nodded and went back through the gate. The gate swung open with a metallic whine and the guard waved them in. The gate clanged shut behind them as they drove up the concrete driveway towards a porch that sheltered the main entrance to the house.

A man wearing a slate grey salwar and long shirt stood inside the porch. A holstered pistol hung at his waist. As the car stopped near him he came forward and opened the door for Shafiq Ahmed and gave a half salute, and told the driver to park the car on one side beyond the porch. He then escorted Shafiq up the few steps into the house and to a room on the right hand side. It was a largish room with a lot of padded chairs along the walls and a number of richly upholstered sofa chairs on an inner circle. Two large chandeliers hung over the huge Kashmiri carpet spread in the middle, partly covering the marble tiled floor.

Shafiq stood just inside the door, taking in the lavishly furnished room. His escort left him there and proceeded to the far end of the room where some men were standing. Shafiq realised that Abdul Gani Shah sat there, on a low throne-like couch, surrounded by a number of persons who were conferring with him in muted voices. The escort whispered to him, gesturing towards the door. Abdul Gani Shah immediately looked towards Shafiq standing near the door, and motioned to the people around him to leave the room. Only the armed escort who had brought Shafiq in remained, standing behind and to one side of Shah. Shah got up from his couch and padded across the carpet towards Shafiq saying "*Khush Amdeed*, welcome. Good to see you after such a long time. How are you?" He came up to Shafiq and enveloped him in a warm hug, then motioned to him to join him at the end of the room where he had been sitting.

Shafiq was a little taken aback by this warm and effusive welcome and responded nervously with a more formal, "*Salam-e-leykum*, Abdul Gani Shah sahib. It was very gracious of you to accede so promptly to my request for a meeting—considering that you must have a busy schedule." Then he added, "I hope you and your family are in good health?"

Abdul Gani Shah settled down on his couch and motioned to Shafiq to sit in the sofa chair near him, then said with a jocular air, "What is all this formality you are observing? I am no sahib-wahib for you—or are you trying to negate our old friendship? As to busy schedule, do we not all have that in our businesses? But there is always time for old friends." He motioned to the guard standing behind him and whispered to him to tell someone to bring refreshments. Then turning back to Shafiq asked, "So how is business? Prospering as usual? I hear that the saffron crop is going to be good this year, so you should have a good trade on that side."

"You are right Shah sah . . . , sorry, Abdul Gani, we should have a good saffron crop this year, and since I buy a lot of the crop for processing and subsequent trade, it should help to balance off the drop of sales of handicrafts and carpets that we have experienced due to low tourist arrivals." Shafiq was surprised that his host and friend knew about his business and involvement in saffron trading.

"You know Shafiq," Abdul Gani replied, "you should not rely so much on these miserly Indian tourists for your sales. Try to export. What is your son doing now? He must be old enough to join you in your business?"

"That's right. He finished school earlier this year, and I told him no college-follege. That is for clerks and people who want to serve others; you work with me, help me expand my business. He is working with me now and I hope that he can soon help me in opening a showroom in India, so that we can sell to foreign tourists all the year round."

"Good, good," Abdul Gani said. "With Allah's blessings he will be successful. Ah! Here are some refreshments to keep our stomachs from grumbling while we chat," he said as a servant rolled in a trolley laden with snacks and beverages. After they had filled their plates and glasses, he continued, "So tell me, what made you suddenly remember your old friend after such a long time?"

"I don't know if it was right of me," Shafiq began hesitantly, "but there was a small problem . . . and I thought you might be able to do something to help."

Abdul Gani looked at him with a level, appraising gaze and said, "If Allah is willing, and it is within my power, I will definitely try to help. So do not hesitate—tell me what the problem is."

Shafiq had been a bit cowed down by his friend's fort-like establishment and his 'darbar' like drawing room, but he picked up courage now to complete the task he had come for. He took a sip of his drink and putting his glass on the side table, began, "The problem is not to do with my family, or my business—that is all well by the grace of god. I have come to intercede on behalf of another family that is in trouble—a family of Kashmiri Pandits living in the Habba Kadal area." He noticed a frown of annoyance on his host's brow and stopped for a moment; then again picking up courage continued by way of explanation. "My son, Bashir, and this boy Roshan in that family, have been very close friends for over ten years, and Bashir pleaded with me to try to help them."

Abdul Gani Shah did not say anything, but his frown of annoyance seemed to have deepened. He curtly gestured to Shafiq to continue. Shafiq was now decidedly uncomfortable, but continued hurriedly with his story of that family's travails, and how the situation had been deteriorating over the last week—ending with last night's incident of open threats. Having finished his tale he sat forward on the edge of his sofa chair, looking anxiously at Abdul Gani. The atmosphere was decidedly tense now, and all the bonhomie his friend had shown earlier had completely evaporated.

There was a long period of uneasy silence. It was apparent from Abdul Gani's tight lipped expression that he was angry. He was trying to control his emotions so that his anger did not burst forth and overwhelm his friend. When he spoke a few minutes later he seemed to have composed himself and his voice was calm. "You remember Shafiq, in school, in the fourth class, we had a teacher named Raina. I know that I was not so good at studies, but he seemed to pick me out every day, for some mistake or the other, and hit me on the knuckles with his thick wooden ruler. It hurt a lot, and I was very happy and relieved when the year ended and we moved on to the next class. I thought that I would finally escape Raina's punishment.

"But that was not to be. In the fifth class the teacher was Kaul, and his form of punishment was the twisting of ears. He would grip my ear between his thumb and forefinger and wrench my head back and forth till I thought my ear would come out. The pain was excruciating and lasted longer—and in no way helped me to become a better student. It only embedded in me a deep loathing for the Pandits, who seemed to dominate the teaching fraternity. I eventually dropped out of school and to avoid constant bickering from my father, took a job as a conductor on an inter-city bus service. I was happy then, travelling from place to place and free as a bird. But at the end of every month I had to go to the office to collect my meager salary from—guess who? Triloki Nath, the head accountant, who glared malevolently at me over his half-frame spectacles and handed me my pay almost grudgingly—but always with some deductions for one reason or the other.

"I was thirteen or fourteen years old at that time—an impressionable age. I started wondering why it was the Pandits who held all the crucial positions in all organisations. A few years later, when I joined the Kashmir Transport Employees Union, I came across a number of politically motivated persons. Through association with them I finally unraveled the mystery that had rankled in my mind all those years. Our State had been ruled by Hindu kings for many generations. It was natural for them to trust the Pandits with all the important administrative jobs, rather than the Muslims. And even though the Muslims proliferated more rapidly and became the majority community in the valley, they never really gained favour with the Maharajas. The Pandits had dug their roots so deep that they continue to dominate even today, though the new governments have Muslims as the Chief Ministers and Ministers."

He stopped for breath, and Shafiq thought that it was an opportunity for him to put in a word. He hesitantly murmured, "Abdul Gani sahib, I am sorry to interrupt, but I would just like to say that I do not see why an honest middle-class *kirana* shopkeeper should be made to suffer, just because some others from his community have played a dominant role in ruling the State in the past—as you have so succinctly explained just now? Maybe some Pandits have been conniving and have spread their community's web through important jobs in the Government and other services, but should the whole community be pilloried for that reason? A large number of them earn an honest living through their shrewd business sense or better education. If our own boys showed equal zeal and commitment, I am sure that they would have no cause for complaint."

The dam of Abdul Gani's patience seemed to break and he retorted angrily, "You are a fool Shafiq! A snake is always a snake! It might lie dormant and peaceful for a long time, seemingly harmless, but its venom just builds up inside till it strikes again. We can never hope to achieve the full freedom on our fields and meadows while these snakes lie curled up in the grass, or in their burrows. To achieve our objective of freedom from infidel rule in the valley we have to root out all these vermin."

His anger seemed to ebb a little and he continued in a more composed, reasonable voice, "Tell me Shafiq, when there is a cricket or hockey match being shown on the television, where the Indian and Pakistan teams are playing against each other, who do you and your son root for in your heart of hearts?"

Shafiq thought for a moment, then mumbled, "Pakistan I suppose."

"Exactly," Abdul Gani said triumphantly; then asked, "and who do you think those Pandits and others cheer for?"

"India," Shafiq muttered almost under his breath.

"So you see?" Abdul Gani said with a look of satisfaction, as if sealing a debate. "Then we *are* on opposite sides in this battle for supremacy in the valley; and if we have to win the battle we have to eliminate the enemy. I am in constant contact with the Pakistani authorities and they have offered full support for our cause, if we are able to decimate the non-Muslims in the valley. They rightly say that once this is achieved, it will strengthen our hands in achieving 'aazadi' from the infidel rule. The infiltrating mujahedin have already achieved fair success in cleansing the villages. They have full support from our FSP cadres located there. Now that we have found that the CRP and JKP are in a weak and inadequate position to confront them, and that the Indian army is unable to provide them support for internal security, we have to make our move to push forward the movement in the smaller towns and in Srinagar. The ISI and the Pakistani army have promised all support once we have achieved initial success."

"My friend," Shafiq said in a soft, measured tone, "you are obviously more shrewd and conversant with such political strategies. I can only say that it is dangerous to keep company with jackals. They are only interested in their lump of meat. I hope that that is not what they are looking for in our beautiful valley. From what I have learnt, they have already reduced what they call 'Azad' Kashmir to serfdom. The people there are in a miserable condition, totally crushed under the iron heel of the army. I would hate to see the same fate overtake us." Shafiq got up from his chair, realising that he had inadvertently come to the lion's den to plead mercy for a lamb. "I must not take up more of your precious time," he said to Abdul Gani Shah, "I hope that you will pardon me for my ignorance in matters concerning the welfare of our valley and its people. I thank you for enlightening me. May Allah's mercy ever be on you."

"And on you too, my friend," Abdul Gani said without any warmth of feeling and making no effort to get up from his seat. He motioned to his guard, "See our honoured guest out to his car." When Shafiq was almost near the door, Abdul Gani called out, "By the way, what is the name of this Pandit family in Habba Kadal?"

"They are the Bhans. The son's name is Roshan Bhan. They live somewhere along the second street." Shafiq called back; then gesturing a final salaam he left the room followed by his escort.

After the sound of the departing car had faded away, the guard returned to the room. "Call Shamsuddin," Abdul Gani commanded tersely. The person soon entered the room and bowed to Abdul Gani, who spoke to him in a low voice for a few minutes. After a while he said to him in dismissal, "See to it that it is done tonight. I do not want to hear that name again at dawn."

He leaned back in his couch with a sigh of satisfaction, then asked his guard to call back the others who had been in conference with him earlier.

ROSHAN'S TALE

Roshan and his friend Sunil Vohra sat under the shade of some trees on the bank of the Jammu Canal, sipping beer from their bottles. It was autumn and though the heat had subsided, the humidity level was high. Roshan had recently purchased a second-hand scooter and the two friends decided to move out of the congestion and claustrophobia of the city to the relative coolness of the Canal Road. They did this whenever they had a day off and neither of them had a host of household chores to catch up on.

The two had met a couple of years back, after Roshan had got a job as Accountant with the Indian Institute of Integrated Science, where Sunil was already working as a Research Assistant. They were both bachelors in their late twenties and found that they had a lot in common. Since the IIIS was situated a little off Canal Road they sometimes spent time on the canal banks eating *pakoras* bought from a roadside tea stall, before they went to their respective homes in the evening. Roshan often joked that this drain of a canal was the nearest thing to his beloved Jhelum that he could find near Jammu—and therefore his favourite spot for relaxation. Of course the Tawi River was also swollen after the monsoons, but its abundance was too brief and its rocky banks were bereft of greenery and shade.

Today Sunil could feel that Roshan was in a pensive mood. As he quietly sipped his beer, his eyes seemed to stare unseeingly into the foliage on the opposite bank of the canal, and his mind was focused even further away. The water in the canal was clear and sparkled in the sunlight, free from the sewage and waste water that normally polluted the Tawi River. A cool breeze caressed the water and ruffled the leaves of the trees and bushes along the banks. It was peaceful here.

Sunil waited for a while for Roshan to break out of his reverie then asked impatiently, "What's the matter Roshan, why are you so lost in thought?"

Roshan sighed deeply, then plucking at the grass near him said in a choked voice, as if to himself, "She would have been twenty-five today." He broke off, tears welling up in his eyes as he looked at the ground.

Sunil was startled and looked with concern at his friend. "What happened? Who are you talking about?"

Roshan was quiet for a few minutes, then murmured, "Rohini, my sister."

Sunil looked silently at the water rushing by in the canal. Though they had been friends for a couple of years, there was not much that he knew about Roshan's family, except that they were Kashmiri Pandits who had migrated from the valley and that they lived in a dilapidated house in one of the poorer suburbs of Jammu. There was never any mention of siblings—till now. Sunil waited, uncertain of what he should do. Roshan seemed to be so emotionally charged that he did not want to disturb his peace of mind further by asking questions that might be delicate—insensitive. Then again, he thought, it might actually help if he were to break through this wall of reserve that was bottling up Roshan's emotions within him. That was what friendship was all about: sharing in happiness and sorrow, not just sipping beer together along the banks of the canal.

He plucked up courage and asked gently, "Tell me Roshan, tell me about Rohini, about your family. You have never talked to me about your past life. What made you leave Kashmir to come and settle here? Was it to do with all that trouble that erupted there eight-nine years back?"

"Ten . . . ten years back," Roshan corrected him absent-mindedly, still lost in his thoughts. "She was so beautiful," he continued, his voice mellowing in recollection. "Fair, as all Pandit girls are; with rosy cheeks and grey-green eyes that sparkled with mischief when she was in a playful mood. So . . . so innocent. Just fourteen then; in fact we were thinking of how we should celebrate her approaching fifteenth birthday. But it was not to be." Roshan's voice choked as he sobbed silently, the tears now flowing freely down his cheeks.

Sunil got up and sat closer to Roshan, putting his arm around his shoulders. After a little while Roshan's sobs subsided and his shuddering body quietened. He straightened up and taking out his handkerchief blew his nose vigorously. "Thanks," he mumbled as he wiped his face and eyes.

Sunil waited for Roshan to compose himself, then said softly, "Now tell me. It will help to ease the pain in your heart if you try to unburden yourself."

"You know, there are so many clichés one hears," Roshan said sardonically, "the biggest ones are that time is the big healer, and that sharing halves one's pain. But some gashes are so deep that they seem to take a life-time to heal—if at all. I've heard that long after an arm or a leg is amputated, the brain still sends signals to the ends from which it was severed, making the person feel as if it were still there. Only the evidence of the eyes lays bare the reality of the loss. With me there is no physical deformity to grieve over; the wounds are all buried deep inside—festering sores that refuse to go away. The loss of my sister, the loss of my friends, the loss of my birth place and legacy, and more than anything, the loss of faith in humanity—the loss of humanity itself; where does one go—who does one turn to for solace, for healing?"

Roshan paused and looked at Sunil, "I'm sorry. I'm being unfair to you. I suppose when one encounters lack of civility for a long period of time it rubs off on one's psyche."

Roshan took a long gulp from his bottle of beer and lay back on the grass, staring into the pale blue sky above. "Ten years back we were a happy family of four: me, my parents and my little sister," he began. "And I had two very dear friends who had been with me throughout our schooling and afterwards. Life flowed so peacefully that there seemed to be no scope for turmoil. O there was turmoil all around us—what with terrorists and fundamentalists and separatists and so on—but it did not touch us in our daily lives; except for the occasional curfews and calls for *hartal*.

"It was just after I had joined college that things started to show signs of change; a change that was so weird in the context of the culture of the valley that it appeared bizarre. For generations all communities in the valley had lived in harmony. True our faiths were different and our living styles and eating habits, but these were mutually accepted and respected. We all lived as one non-communal community. That is where the change started taking place—and the pace at which it was happening was bizarre. The alienation was seeded in spring and it exploded in autumn. It appeared as if an invisible hand had hovered over the valley and covered it with its dark shadow.

"I felt the tremors rather late, probably because I was too keen to provide justification for everything: unwilling to impute evil motives to anything strange that happened. But all this I can say now, in retrospect. When I look back, I can see everything happening in slow motion; a tsunami approaching on the horizon appears to be just a harmless ripple. The initial teasing and taunts and seemingly harmless aggression soon converted to open threats. If we had acted sooner Rohini might have been alive today, celebrating her birthday with us.

"On the previous night a group of boys had thrown stones on our tin roof creating a racket. In response to my shouted protest and threat of calling the police, they shouted back counter threats: asking us to leave the valley. But what was even worse, they said that we should leave the women behind for them to take care off. The innuendo was shocking, filthy. Though their faces were not discernible in the dark, it was apparent that these were the same neighbourhood boys who had been pestering us for weeks. That they should now stoop so low was beyond understanding. My father and I were standing at our window and heard all this; but the racket had been so loud that I am sure that everyone in our house heard their parting comments.

"A week earlier I had talked to my friend Ravi about the trouble we were facing, and he had promised to seek assistance for us from a senior contact he knew in the police. With no sign of Ravi, and with this more serious threat that night, I decided to approach my other friend, Bashir, to see if he could help. The local police had waived off our complaints saying it was just boys playing pranks. My father was just a small *kirana* shopkeeper and we did not have any notable contacts. These friends were from more affluent families, more likely to have contacts at a higher level. I fervently hoped that they could come to our rescue. But that was not to be.

"That afternoon, after talking to Bashir, I went to my father's shop to help him out with his accounts and inventories. Then we closed the shop early, so that we could be home well before dark. We were all subdued after the events of the previous night, and had an early dinner and retired to our rooms to occupy ourselves with reading, or doing small chores. We lived in a small, narrow, two-storied house. My room was on the first floor facing the front, with a storeroom next to it, and Rohini's room was behind mine. Our parents lived on the ground floor, and there was a kitchen at the back and our living room in front.

"Sleep was not easy to come by, but I must have fallen off into a fitful sleep sometime late at night. When I woke up it was well past midnight. I could smell something burning, a sort of mixed wood and kerosene smell like you get when lighting a camp fire. I got out of bed and went towards the staircase outside my room. I was halfway down the stairs when I realised that there was a lot of smoke swirling up the stairs. Through the open door of the living room I could see flames licking at the curtains and furniture. As I stood there, momentarily stunned, there was a crash of glass and a bottle came flying into the room, spilling liquid that immediately fanned the fury of the existing flames. I shouted to my parents that the house was on fire and they should get out immediately. Then I climbed back up the stairs to wake up Rohini.

"Fortunately, the fire was still contained within the living room, which was separated from the staircase and the passage to the front door by a wall, so we were all able to get out of the house within ten minutes, despite the fact that smoke was now billowing all over the house. But those old houses in Srinagar are like tinderboxes: mainly wood and brick structures that are highly combustible. By the time we reached the lane outside our house the flames were climbing up the walls and licking the first floor. A large number of our neighbours had also collected on the lane outside and someone said that they had called the fire brigade. A little away from us, towards the end of the lane, a small group of people were standing in the dark, whispering among themselves.

"What happened next is firmly etched in my mind. Rohini looked down the lane, then broke away from us and rushed towards the house, her night-dress billowing behind her, shouting, 'I must get my clothes.' It took me a while to register what was happening and then I ran after her shouting to her to come back. By the time I reached the front door she was already half-way up the stairs. I could hardly see her because of the thick smoke. Suddenly a huge flash of flame leapt out of the living room door and engulfed the staircase. The heat was so intense that I staggered back and rushed out to the front of the house, shouting to Rohini to come back. She appeared for a moment at the window of my bedroom as if waving goodbye to us; then the flames engulfed the whole front of the house. We could only hear the crackling of the fire intermingled with Rohini's screams of agony. After a while all that remained were the cracking sounds of timber and glass as we watched the flames pluming over the house in stunned silence.

"The fire brigade arrived an hour later, to douse the embers of the charred skeleton of the house. The police also arrived and they bundled us into a van to carry us away. In response to our protests they explained that over a dozen Pandit houses had been burnt down all over the old city that night; it was not safe for us to remain there.

"I have often wondered why Rohini ran into the burning house. She was not a child who did not understand the implication of her action. Perhaps she did it deliberately in reaction to the previous night's innuendoes? Perhaps she saw in the dark figures down the lane that night a threat? One will never know.

"What more is there to say? We were taken that night to a Police Station where we were given blankets to protect us from the cold. The next morning we were transported to a make-shift camp beyond the cantonment area, where a large number of Pandit families were lodged—some from villages and some from the city. No one was allowed to go outside the camp. A week later, on some bureaucrat or politician's decree, we were put into buses and transported to Jammu like caged birds.

"I can feel now the agony of an uprooted tree. It becomes just a log: with no identity, no name; just a species-less non-being. It took a year for my father to establish his credentials with his bank, so that he could access his existing account from their Jammu branch. Till then we lived out of a tent in the refugee camp established for us on the periphery of the city, surviving on the sporadic largesse of the government department made responsible for our welfare. We were refugees in our own country, our own State. Fortunately, before their sympathy could peter out, father was able to draw some money from his bank account—his life's savings—and he rented a small house in a suburb, and invested some of the money for starting a small *kirana* shop operating out of the room facing the lane outside our house.

"After protracted correspondence with my former school in Srinagar I was able to get an authenticated copy of my school leaving certificate. With that in hand I could restart my education, with evening classes in a local college. During the day I tried to sell insurance policies, after pleading and cajoling with one of the firms to let me have an agency. It wasn't easy, because there were swarms of us descending upon the local business community or middle class citizens seeking the same slice of cake. The term 'Kashmiri Pandit refugee' was an epithet that we were tagged with, with repugnance, in the city.

"Anyway, five years back I finally got my B. Com. degree and started looking for a proper job." Roshan sat up and dusted the grass off the back of his tee shirt; then taking a long swig from his now warm beer, he said, "So here I am now, sitting on the banks of this tiny canal, drinking warm beer and boring a patient friend with my story."

Before Sunil could say anything he added, "But let me tell you Sunil, I am not thankless for what I have. I have been given a second chance in life and I plan to make the most of it. As soon as I get my promotion in a few months, I plan to move my parents to a better house; to ease some of the burden from my father's shoulders. We cannot wallow in our miseries forever and must move on, and up. That is what life is all about. Perhaps we will come back again to this canal bank next year, on this day. We will drink beer and give remembrance to Rohini's birthday. Perhaps I will grieve for her as much as I do today, and still wonder where my two friends are—who were not there in my time of need. But at least the beer will not get warm and my story would have got cold." Roshan got up and drained the last drops from his bottle. "Let us go and get something to eat, I am famished."

They got onto the scooter and headed for the city. Behind them two empty beer bottles rolled slowly down the slope and plopped into the canal—to float away to another world.

THE SEARCH

When Ravi reached Ahmed Joy & Sons, Bashir was busy attending to some customers. He saw Ravi through the door and signaled to him that he would be out in a moment. He came out of the shop five minutes later muttering "miserly Indians, they will see a hundred things and then buy a handkerchief."

Ravi refused to be drawn into that argument but thought, 'thank your stars that you have a customer; with all the trouble in the valley the tourists have all vanished.' Instead he asked, "Have you seen Roshan?"

Bashir retorted angrily, "Where have you been for a week. Indeed I have seen Roshan, but that was two days back. He was distraught and told me all about his problems. He said that you had promised to try and help him out, but then you just disappeared. Anyway, I told him that I would see if I could help. It seems that the previous night those rowdies who had been troubling him and his family threw stones on their roof and made all sort of nasty threats. Roshan was really agitated, so I talked to my father to see if he knew anyone who could help. But my father has not said anything to me about it since then, and Roshan hasn't come to see me either; even though he was supposed to meet me yesterday."

"I've just been to college," Ravi said. "He hasn't been there for a few days and no one has seen him. I think we should try and check out what has happened. Perhaps we should go to his father's shop in Maisuma Bazar."

"Yes, that's a good idea," Bashir said. "Wait, my father is not here, I'll just tell my assistants that I'll be back in an hour." He went inside the shop and then came out in five minutes shrugging on a fancy synthetic jacket.

They walked briskly down Residency Road. "Where have you been in any case?" Bashir asked. "Did you go out of town? Roshan said that he hadn't seen you for a week—and neither have I. And he said that he had walked past your house in Wazir Bagh and it seemed as if there was no one there—all the windows were shut."

"No, no," Ravi said brusquely, wanting to steer away from the subject, especially now that he knew the full reason behind their moving to Shivpura. "Father wanted to get the house repainted before winter set in, so he thought it would be wiser to move out to the Shivpura house while that was being done. I was busy helping out with the shifting; I didn't even go to college for the past week."

"So you have no idea of what has been happening in the city for the last couple of days?" Bashir said, almost accusingly. "I believe that there has been a lot of trouble in the old city and many houses have been set on fire by terrorists."

"Now that you mention that," Ravi said thinking back, "there was a grey cloud over the sky down river when I was walking along the Bund to college this morning. I wondered what the reason could be; it seemed so incongruous against the clear morning sky. It must have been the smoke rising from the remnants of one of those fires you are talking about."

They had reached Maisuma by this time and started looking for the signboard proclaiming 'Bhan Provision Store'. They finally located it but the shutters were down. They asked at the neighbouring shop and were told that no one had come to open the shop for the last two days. In fact the two boys who helped 'Bhan sahib' with work at the shop had come in the morning on both days, and then gone away disappointed by mid-morning when no one came to open the shop.

As they were talking to the shopkeeper, a boy came up to them and asked whether they were enquiring about 'Bhan sahib'. When they confirmed that they were, the boy said that he was one of the assistants at his shop. In fact he was going to visit 'Bhan sahib's' residence just now to check why he had not come for the last two days. He knew where the residence was because he was often asked by 'Bhan sahib' to deliver provisions to the house. The boy asked if they would like to accompany him. Ravi and Bashir agreed and Bashir suggested that they take a scooter rickshaw so that he could go back to his shop as soon as possible.

Fifteen minutes later they were in the second lane behind the main street from Habba Kadal. The boy who had escorted them told the scooter driver to stop near a small gate down the lane. He hopped off and opened the gate, then almost staggered back. Ravi and Bashir also got off the rickshaw and told the driver to wait. They went around the half open gate and came to a sudden stop, aghast at what they saw. Before them stood the charred remains of what had once been a house. Through the open spaces between the blackened, roofless walls, where the doors and windows had been on the upper floor, the pale sky peeped through, as if to emphasize the fact that all life had fled.

After staring at this scene for a little while Ravi placed a hand on the boy's shoulder and asked in a hoarse voice, "Are you sure this is the right house?"

The boy replied in a hushed voice, "Yes, this was."

Bashir suggested in a mute voice, "Perhaps we should check with the neighbours what happened? Maybe they will know where the family has gone?"

Ravi nodded in assent but did not move, still staring transfixed at the charred remains of the house. The scooter driver asked impatiently if they were going to be there for long, and Bashir signaled to him in irritation to wait, before going down the lane to the next gate. He unlatched the gate and went down the short path and knocked on the front door. From the narrow oblong window to one side of the door a curtain was shifted surreptitiously and a pair of eyes peeped out fearfully; then the curtain dropped back into place. Bashir was about to knock again when he heard the squeak of a bolt being drawn inside and the door opened a crack. A young, girlish voice asked, "What do you want? Who are you?"

"My name is Bashir. I am a friend of Roshan Bhan who lived next door. I came to meet him but their house seems to have burnt down. Do you know what happened? Where they have gone?"

The door opened a little bit more and Bashir could see that there was a small boy, some seven-eight years old, standing inside, looking apprehensively at him, as if wondering whether he should talk to him or shut the door. Bashir smiled gently at him and said, "Don't worry, I won't harm you. I only want to know what happened—if you know."

The boy took as step forward, appraising Bashir, but still blocking the partly open door. Then he said hesitantly, "They came that night and burnt the house down."

Bashir thought for a moment then asked, "Who, the boys from the neighbourhood?"

The boy wagged his head vigorously from side to side and said, "No, it was big men in dark *phirans*. I live in the room upstairs and had just got up to do so-so when I heard some sound from outside. I peeped outside through the window to see if anyone was coming into our house. I saw three men enter the gate next door and go towards the front windows. They threw some things inside the window and then rushed out of the gate. After a little while there were lots of flames and smoke and everyone shouted fire fire and Abba said that we must all go to the lane outside in case the fire spread to our house and we did." He stopped for breath since he had become more and more excited as he talked. "I saw it all!" he ended importantly. "But Abba said not to talk about it to anyone, so don't tell anyone I told you."

"Don't worry, I won't tell anyone," Bashir assured him. "You are a brave boy. Tell me, did you see anything more; do you know what happened to the Bhans?"

The boy screwed up his nose and eyes, thinking hard, then said, "I am very sad about Rohini *didi*."

"Rohini *didi*?" Bashir asked, puzzled.

"Oho! Roshan *bhaya's* sister," the boy said, irritated at this person's lack of knowledge. "They always told me to call them *bhaya* and *didi*—and I did. Rohini *didi* was so sweet, she always brought toffees for me and told me so many stories."

"So what happened to Rohini *didi*, why are you so sad about her?" Bashir asked.

"We were all standing in the lane, and then she suddenly ran into the burning house and never came out. Ammi says she went to God. I was so frightened that I went to pee into the gutter further down the lane where no one could see me. While I was doing that I heard someone saying, 'Come on Shamsuddin bhai let us go. Shah sahib will be happy.' And these men went away and I ran back to Ammi. Then the fire truck came and Roshan bhaya and his Ammi and Abba sat in a police jeep and went away, and Abba said we could go back into our house now that there was no danger from the fire."

"You are a clever boy," Bashir said, patting him on the head, "what . . ."

"Rasool! What are you doing at the door! Go in at once!" a woman shrieked from behind Bashir.

Bashir turned around and saw a plump woman in a *phiran* coming through the gate. He went towards her and said, "Please don't scold your son, he is a sweet boy. I am Bashir, Roshan Bhan's friend. I came to meet him and saw their house burnt. I was just trying to find out if anyone knew where the family has gone."

"We don't know," the woman said curtly, "the police took them away after the fire. We don't want to talk about it, so go away." She went inside and bolted the door. Bashir could hear her loudly admonishing her son as he walked towards the gate.

Roshan and the shop assistant were waiting quietly for him as he came out of the gate and latched it. "Let's go," Bashir said in a grim voice, "there is nothing more we can do here. I will tell you what I found out when we get back."

The rickshaw driver was happy to be on the way again. As they reached the end of the lane he turned slightly and said over his shoulder, "Pandit house hunh? At least ten more Pandit houses have been burnt down in the past two days in this area alone. It is like an epidemic. I hear that all Pandits are now fleeing from Kashmir fearing for their lives. A pity, they are not bad people. Don't know why some people have turned against them."

He lapsed into silence as they entered the heavy traffic on the main road. Bashir and Ravi dropped off the shop assistant at Budshah Chowk and went on to Linking Road.

That evening the government decided to clamp curfew over the entire city for the night. It looked like the two previous night's incidents had made it realise that they were no longer able to control the situation, and that it was liable to escalate further if they did not take immediate measures. Bashir had told Ravi what he had found out from the boy in the next house that morning, and they had decided that they would go to the police station in Habba Kadal that evening and make further enquiries about the whereabouts of the Bhan family. But now they were not in a position to put their plan in action.

Ravi went to his father's shop, so that they could go back home together after closing the shop before the curfew came into effect. Bashir and his father did the same. By the time darkness fell, an ominous silence had descended over the city, except for the dogs barking in endless conversation through the night.

On the way home, Ravi conveyed to his father the sketchy information they had been able to garner about the tragedy at the Bhan's house two nights back. Ramdev Chandra decided that he would call up Rashid Ahmed and try to get further information. But Rashid was not able to help much. He said that they were aware of the burning of Pandit houses all over the old city, and that they had got information about plans for large scale rioting; which was why curfew had been imposed. Simultaneously they had removed all affected Pandit families to a temporary camp just beyond the cantonment, so that they did not come to further harm. But it would be impossible to get information about individual families in the camp. For one thing, there was total chaos in the camp, secondly there were numerous Bhans and Rainas and Kauls in the camp and there was no way they could locate one family even if the father's full name were known. Ravi and his father slept uneasy that night, wondering whether they could have avoided this tragedy if they had not been so self-centered in the welfare of their own family, and so strict in shielding the secret information provided to them by Rashid.

Bashir too had narrated to his father the story of their visit to Habba Kadal as they made their way home that evening. His father listened in silence till he came to the end of his narration of what the small boy had said. His ears pricked up and he asked, "What did you say? What did the boy say about what those men in the dark lane were saying?"

Bashir looked at him quizzically, then repeated, ". . . that Shah sahib would be happy."

"Oh God!" Shafiq Ahmed said in agitation, "what have I done!" He then told Bashir about his visit to Abdul Gani Shah, ostensibly to seek help for the Bhan family. He related how he had slowly realised during their conversation that he had come to the wrong person. "As I was leaving," Shafiq Ahmed said, "he asked me who I had come pleading for. I was taken by surprise and made the mistake of giving him the name and the approximate location of their house. I should have realized that the FSP was part of this whole conspiracy." He lapsed into a guilty, repentant silence.

"No Abba," Bashir consoled him. "It was not your fault. This was all pre-planned: pre-ordained. It was just a question of who came first and who came next in their scheme of things. Their's was not the only house burnt down—there were countless others. Their conspiracy was much too deep-rooted to be affected by your visit."

"But still . . ." Shafiq said, then became silent. His mind churned with the thought of that poor little girl;

she had probably immolated herself out of fright at what might happen to her at the hands of those boys. Then he thought of his young daughters at home. His conscience refused to pardon him.

∞

UNEASY CALM

The city rested for three days. With the curfew on there was no traffic on the roads except for the occasional police or army vehicles cruising by. No noise, no pollution; even the birds chirped in subdued voices. Only the dogs carried on with their interminable routine conversations, unmindful of the change.

By the third day stomachs began to rumble as rations dwindled in the kitchen and vegetables disappeared altogether. Beggars and daily wage labourers felt the pinch most, their hand-to-mouth living leaving them without even the buffer of stray crumbs. So did the farmers whose vegetables rotted since they were unable to move them to the hungry city. The shopkeepers had their Associations and Unions, as did the hotel and houseboat and taxi owners, which had strong lobbies. They themselves might not have grumbled too much for another couple of days of enforced holiday during this off season, but their wives goaded them into action. They finally conveyed their complaints to the politicians who constantly came to them for funds or sought their votes. Ignoring the advice of the security forces and the army, the government finally acquiesced and allowed a partial, five hour relaxation on the fourth day. Everything sprung into frenzied action before the doors of freedom clanged shut again.

While Gurbax Singh went hunting for vegetables, Ravi borrowed his father's car to initiate an investigation of his own. Since they were living next to the cantonment area he decided to go hunting for the camp where the Pandits were supposed to have been corralled. Though he managed to locate the camp, it was almost deserted. From the sentries standing guard at the gate of the fenced in enclosure, he got the information that most of the 'inmates' of the camp had been put onto buses and moved to Jammu during the past two days. The few that remained were the last arrivals, and they were just waiting for more buses to be arranged. Ravi turned back disappointed.

Since he had a few hours on hand before he had to return home, he decided to go into the city. Even though the curfew had been lifted most of the shops were closed; there was no point in opening them for such a short period. Only the shops peddling groceries and vegetables and household goods were open, and they were doing brisk business. Ravi drove down Residency Road, through Lal Chowk and over Amira Kadal, before heading back home down Maulana Azad Road. This was the centre of town but the streets wore a deserted look, with police pickets outnumbering the citizens on the roads. As he turned into the driveway of their Shivpura house he could hear the first sirens going on, signaling that the curfew would be effective again shortly.

Now that he had learnt that all the Pandits at the camp had been moved to Jammu, Ravi at least had the assurance that Roshan and his parents would not come to further harm. At the same time it meant that they were one step further away from being located and contacted by him. He felt an emptiness at this loss—and an even more agonising pain at the thought of what had befallen his friend in terms of the loss he had suffered. Combined with that was the uncertainty of when they would be able to come back, if at all, given the circumstances of their departure and the pall of gloom that had enveloped the valley.

Over the next few days the curfew was relaxed further, for progressively longer periods during daytime, even as night curfew continued to be in force. An increasing number of shops started opening up for limited periods, even though commerce revolved basically around essential commodities. By late afternoon everyone would be scampering around to close shop and pull down the shutters so that they could reach home well before dark. It was an uneasy normalcy, imposed by heavy police patrolling along the main arteries of the city. There was nervousness in the air, a shocked disbelief as news percolated through the city about the disaster that had struck the Pandit community.

By the beginning of the following week schools and colleges started opening and Ravi began leaving the house early, with the car that went to drop Savita off to school. From there he would walk along the Bund to his college. Even though the morning walk in the crisp cool air invigorated him, the passage past their Wazir Bagh house always depressed him and brought back to his mind thoughts of the unintended betrayal of trust of his friend. The atmosphere in the college was none too congenial. The Pandit boys had all gone away and there was only a sprinkling of non-Muslim students remaining there: basically the Sikhs and other Punjabis. They felt a defensive awkwardness in that environment, as if anticipating that they would be the next targets of attack: of the flushing out operation that had overtaken the Pandits.

It was a week after Ravi had rejoined college that it happened. Following his normal routine, he had just walked through Wazir Bagh and was at the Gogji Bagh crossing when two boys accosted him. Then two more boys converged on him, one each from the crossroad from his left and right. It was obviously a pre-planned manoeuvre and he was surrounded.

"Yes?" Ravi asked without aggression, surprised at what was happening.

"What yes!" said one of the boys in front of him, who was sporting a thick beard. "Don't you think you have studied enough? You should now be seeing the world. Or would you prefer to see something beyond?"

Ravi was now getting angry. Even though he was aware that he was overwhelmingly outnumbered, he refused to be cowed down. "Do you know who I am? I can have you arrested—I have contacts in the JKP," he blustered, trying at the same to time to push past them.

"We know who you are, Ravi Chandra," the man/ boy with the bushy beard said. "The fact is that you do not know who *we* are. We know that you and your father are cowards who ran away from your house down the road. But you will not know who we are when we start living in that house soon—because you will no longer be around," the boy laughed scornfully, pulling out a pistol and pressing it into Ravi's stomach. Ravi was stunned. He had expected a scuffle, or perhaps a punch or two, but not a pistol. However, despite the fact that he was frightened now, he reacted by raising his arms above his head and shouting for help. It was now the turn of the boys to be startled. They started looking around nervously to see if anyone was around who could intervene. Fortunately for Ravi a police patrol jeep happened to turn the corner on to the Gogji Bagh Road about a hundred metres away. The boys saw it and decided to disappear into the side lanes—but not before 'bushy beard' shouted over his shoulder, "Remember, we will be back, if you are back."

Ravi was now no longer in the mood to go on to college. Even though he had attended classes earlier in the week, his mind was not on his studies: he had just been following his schedule mechanically, like a robot. He turned back the way he had come. His father's shop was not too far away, but he was reluctant to go there. It was too early for his father to have come to open the shop, and even if he had come he would be surprised to see Ravi there. In any case Ravi did not want to alarm him by telling him about his experience that morning. It was also too early for Bashir to have come to his shop. He stood near Amira Kadal, wondering where he should go; somewhere where he could sit quietly and gather his thoughts—work out what he should do next. Then an idea struck him and he doubled back the way he had come. He was soon at his Wazir Bagh house, banging at the gate and shouting for Gulla to come and open it.

Gulla came to the gate after a few minutes, grumbling about the early morning intrusion. When Ravi identified himself, Gulla quickly unlocked the gate for him, apologetic, though still grumbling. Ravi had the key to the front door of the house, since he had been involved with the shifting operation. He unlocked the door and climbed the stairs all the way to the second floor. His steps echoed through the empty house as he went to his room facing the front of the house. The room was exactly the way he had left it—not even a layer of dust to indicate that it had been abandoned a few weeks back. He drew up a chair near the closed windows and sat there, his feet propped up on the a window sill. Through the film of dust that encrusted the glass from outside, he could see the snowcapped Pir Panjal mountain range stretching in front of him.

A kaleidoscope of thoughts flashed through his mind—of events past, sad and happy; though even the sad ones had had happy endings: a ray of hope that lit up the darkness. But today? Where was the ray of hope today? What could the future foretell for him? Slowly, as he plunged through the morass of his depressed thoughts, a spark did light up, and slowly expanded into a glow. Why was he so depressed—so pessimistic? Just a few months back he had pontificated to Bashir about the whole new world outside the valley, 'a whole new world offering so much more'.

He got up from his chair, a new determination flowing through his veins. He took a last look through the dusty glass windows at the mountain range. Yes, he would seek out the 'whole new world outside the valley', and see what it had to offer him. He shut the door and walked out of the house.

BOSTON

Ravi looked out through the misted glass of his bedroom window, thinking back on his decision to leave the valley twelve years ago. He'd had a long talk with his father that night, telling him that he was no longer able to concentrate on his studies; he felt he needed to get away if he had to achieve anything in life. He said that he felt guilty about such thoughts because it looked like he was abandoning his family in the time of adversity. He did not say anything about the threat he had received that morning; it would have made his decision seem like a reaction, whereas it was considered, deep-thought.

His father had listened patiently, then seemed lost in his thoughts. "You have nothing to feel guilty about Ravi," he had said. "I agree with you. Besides you were always going to America to do your MBA, this just means you will finish your graduation there as well. We should start looking into possibilities immediately."

America had been a totally new experience for him: sometimes disconcerting, sometimes daunting. 'Yes Bashir,' he thought with a smile, 'a whole new world'. But he had learnt to cope, struggling through his education till he finished his MBA and found a job.

Now he was well established with a marketing firm located on the outskirts of Boston, living in this rented forest hideout in the suburbs. Perhaps he had chosen this house away from the city so that he could stay attuned to what he had left behind so many years back. Maybe that was why, when autumn came and the maple leaves turned from green to yellow to rust, his mind grew restless and his thoughts wandered back to the valley, where he had sat on the banks of the Jhelum with his friends, dreaming up mist enshrouded plans for their futures.

∞

RUMBLINGS OF PROTEST

Abdul Gani Shah was getting nervous. It was now some years since the Pandits had been pushed out of the valley. His Pakistani contacts had promised all help in toppling the government using their network of infiltrators. They had promised that he would head the new government they would install in the valley—in an independent Kashmir. Instead, what had happened was that the government in Delhi had pumped in more army and CRP forces into the valley over the subsequent weeks and the tide of terrorism had been stemmed. Then, slowly, the intruders had been weeded out and decimated. Abdul Gani's influence began to wane over time, and with the mushrooming of other separatist organisations in the valley, the flow of funds to the FSP kept shrinking.

In fact that was a problem with all these organisations: each one vying for a larger piece of the cake dangled at them from across the border. Each one tried to implement new strategies to enhance their image with the high priests across the border. FSP propagated the concept that all films were vulgar and were ruining the morals of the people. They burnt down a few cinema halls and picketed others till they were forced to close down. Most of them had been owned by infidels anyway. Movie watching was forced underground, with sales of video players exploding and video cassettes being peddled on the streets—including a mushrooming of pornographic stuff under the counter.

The JLF took up the issue of liquor sales. Imbibing liquor was against the tenets of Islam they pointed out; a lot of bottles were smashed, while the protesters smuggled away an equal number under their *phirans* after looting the vends. Within weeks all liquor vends across the valley were shut down and the morals of the population were rescued from Satan's door yet again. The transactions that took place in Hades were, of course, sacrosanct and not open for discussion.

The FFP took their cue from there. Ban all music they said—then added hastily, all *Bollywood* songs. This, however, was a little bit of a flop since a lot of the popular film songs had been picturised on the feuding Khans in Mumbai who were the darlings of the youngsters. But some of the aspiring youth groups who had formed rock bands came under the hammer of public morality, especially a girls' band that had become very popular. What infamy! It was unfortunate that two of the members of that band were Bashir's sisters, who had joined college over the previous two years. Salima and Sabah protested vociferously to their father over dinner that evening. "How can these people curtail all our freedom? We are not playing in a discotheque. We only play at inter-college competitions or in our college fetes. And if the boys can form their band groups why can't the girls, especially when we are more talented? This is stupid! There are girl bands all over the world."

Shafiq Ahmed listened to them quietly, an indulgent smile playing over his lips. Ever since that incident of the Pandit girl being burnt, he had grown extra protective of his daughters. Bashir was annoyed when they were allowed to join college. "You didn't allow me to join college," he protested, "then why this discrimination?"

His father patted him on the shoulder, "See how well you are doing at your work; if you had not joined me then, it would have taken you another three years to get started—and for what? A meaningless BA degree? Now you are a successful salesman, and your efforts have helped us survive the adverse conditions here. As for your sisters, you shouldn't be jealous of them. They are such lively girls that it would be a crime keeping them at home. Let them enjoy this freedom till they get married"

Reacting to his daughters Shafiq Ahmed said lightheartedly, "You chose the wrong parents, children. If you had been born to parents somewhere else you might not have had such problems. But here, in Srinagar, we have to follow the local customs and rules."

"We would never find a better Abba and Ammi if we searched all over the world," Salima said affectionately, "but this is so unfair. And this isn't even as if our society is imposing this ban, it is just one of those self-serving social policing groups."

"True, *beti*, but that is life," Shafiq said, "we have to take the bad with the good. Be happy that you are living here, in what is called the heaven on earth."

"More like hell on earth," Sabah mumbled, "ever since those terrorists started coming over the border that is what they have made this place. And all these local toadies who suck up to them are just doing it for the money."

"Now Sabah, that is enough!" said Shafiq sternly, and the conversation ended there.

However, when the MeT decreed a few weeks later that all girls had to wear burqas whenever they left their homes, it was the last straw. The two sisters came back fuming from college and shut themselves up in their room, sulking. Their mother, Sameena, knew them too well to interfere; they would be out soon enough when the hunger pangs consumed them.

"Where are the girls?" Shafiq asked his wife when he returned from work, "the house is so quiet; none of their usual chatter. Is something wrong?"

"One of their tantrums." Sameena answered, amused. "But it must be very serious this time, because they have locked themselves up in their room ever since they came back from college, and haven't even stepped out to sneak some biscuits."

"Okay," Shafiq chuckled, "so put dinner on early. The smell of food will entice the lionesses out of their lair."

Soon afterwards Sameena went to the girls' room and knocked at their door announcing that dinner was ready. Predictably, they came out and headed for the dining table, grumpy faced. Shafiq and Bashir had already helped themselves to the rice and were pouring out the curry and vegetables.

"Abba, you must get us admission into a college in Chandigarh," Salima burst out as she sat down in her usual chair next to him. "We have decided that we don't want to study here."

"Okay, I will do it first thing tomorrow morning," Shafiq said straight-faced, but with a wink to Bashir who was sitting across from him at the table.

Salima looked at him quizzically, her rice laden serving spoon arrested in mid-air. This was not the reaction she had expected at all. Then she realised that her father was putting her on and said, pouting, "No, we are serious. We don't want to stay in this horrible place."

"Oh, but a few days back you said that we were the best Abba and Ammi in the world," Shafiq said with an amused smile, continuing to eat his food. "So why do you want to leave us now? Ah, I know, it must be because of Bashir. I realise that he has not been a very good brother to you, but you must give him a chance to make amends."

"Abba!" Salima said petulantly. "Why don't you ever take us seriously?"

"Okay, I'll do that, but first you start eating. Once the hot curry enters your stomach some of the heat in your head will fly out of your ears." When everyone had started eating, he turned towards her and asked, "So tell me what the matter is now. You seem to have a new issue bothering you every week."

"Not every week Abba," Bashir said, "the last outburst was a few weeks back."

"Bhai!" Salima said glaring at him. Then turning to her father, "It's those MeT chaps—the Mussalman-e whatever. They have issued a *firman* this morning saying that all girls must now wear a burqa when they step out of their houses. We refuse to obey such stupid *firmans*. If they do not like to see our faces why don't they stay inside their houses—off the streets."

"You are right," Bashir said, "This is indeed a serious issue; we must take a stand—do something about these dictatorial orders issued by all and sundry who pose to be the custodians of Islam. They just want to pull us all back into the Middle Ages along with them."

"The problem is Bhai," Sabah said, "that these are all concepts imported from outside; do we really have to follow suit? Do we really have to pull blankets over our heads and curtail all our freedoms instead of leading the free happy life that has been part of the cultural heritage of our valley?"

"Wow!" Bashir said, looking at his sisters with astonishment. "You girls have really grown up!"

"It is that Convent education we got," Salima said mischievously. Then serious again, said, "The problem also is Bhai, that it is a few uneducated mischief mongers who are really dictating terms to everyone in the name of religion. They have made religion their shield against any opposition. All the poor people in the valley—all the farmers and the labourers—they just listen quietly to all this. It does not affect them either way, because all they want is to do an honest day's work to feed their families. And in the cities all the good, honest people just listen quietly because they do not want to confront the mischief makers out of fear, even though they know their cloak of religion is false and self-serving. Unfortunately the good people have pushed themselves into a minority by thinking selfishly—in the singular. If they thought collectively, as a community, they would realize that they are the majority—the people who should be giving directions. That is what democracy was supposed to be all about, till it got corrupted."

"Hey, Salima!" Bashir said, "you are quite an orator. Have you ever thought of fighting an election. The State could certainly do with some honest politicians."

"Fighting is the right word," Salima responded, refusing to be diverted. "That is what elections and politicians are all about; fighting for power—and the money it brings. I refuse to be part of their cock fights."

"Okay, enough," Sameena interrupted. "It is not good for your digestion to make such angry, excited talk while having your meal."

"But Ammi, I thought that such conversation was acidic and that helped to digest the food faster," Sabah said, teasing her mother.

"Arre baba," Sameena said in mock frustration. "No one can win an argument with you children. But, if I may continue with what I was about to say, would you all like to have some *phirni* for dessert? It might sweeten your tempers a little."

There was a collective, happy shout of "Yes!" from all of them and Sameena went into the kitchen to fetch the bowl of *phirni*, while Sabah started clearing the used plates off the table. When Sameena had brought the bowl and everyone had served themselves, Shafiq spoke up.

"I am impressed by how you can think on serious issues that affect our society, even though you might be doing it out of a reaction to things that have affected you personally. I am not sure what I should agree with and what I should not. I agree with you Sabah, about your mention of the cultural heritage of our valley. We have always been a peace loving people with few communal enmities or resentments. What happened to the Pandits was the most traumatic experience for us all—for the community that was banished from their homeland as well as for us who remained behind. What was shameful for us was that we allowed it to happen—that we allowed a section, a minute section, of our society to support those actions. You are probably right in saying that this minute section, these subversive organizations, have the financial backing from across the border. Of course our government is to blame, for allowing them to grow and create an atmosphere that allowed them to prosper; but we, the common people, the good people as you say, are the ones who suffer the most—and we are equally to blame for allowing them to prosper in our midst. It is time that we started doing something—not just waiting for the government to do something. So let us start now, whatever we can do at our level, before the situation gets totally out of control."

Bashir spoke, thoughtful, tentative, "I feel that we must first find out how many other people think like us; whether we can convert the singular, as you call it Salima, into the plural. But how do we go about it?"

"I can start talking to my business friends and fellow members at the Kashmir Chamber," Shafiq said. "And Bashir, you are travelling all over the valley meeting suppliers, why don't you start asking them what their feelings are?"

"Sabah and I could start getting feedback from girls in our college," Salima chipped in excitedly. "In fact we could ask some of our friends to extend the survey to their families and friends and acquaintances. That way we would be able to cover a really wide canvas."

"Good, good," Shafiq said with a satisfied expression. "Sameena, why don't you start probing with all your friends and the housewives in the neighbourhood—then we will have covered all cross-sections of our society? In fact if we can get the housewives on our side we will be really well placed if we have to follow up on this; they are the ones who have the strongest influence on all members of a family."

Shafiq Ahmed looked up and down the table as he finished speaking—like a General concluding a meeting. He stroked his peppering beard in satisfaction and said, "I suggest we all have another round of *phirni*."

Everyone concurred happily.

∞

SUPPORT FOR A CAUSE

Vikramjit Chauhan sat at his bedroom window looking out at the mountain range that spread out in front of him from one end of the horizon to the other. The central snow-capped mountains were turning orange in the dying rays of the sun. It was a sight that never failed to entrance him and he tried, as often as possible, to leave his office in time to watch the sunset, a light shawl draped over his crisp uniform to ward off the chill that crept in with the approaching dusk.

He had now been in Srinagar for a little over three years. By the time he had arrived here the looming threat of terrorist dominance had been warded off, though the trauma of the exodus of the Kashmiri Pandits was still fresh in the minds of the people. But though the crisis had been deflected, the presence of these elements still lingered like little pockmarks all over the valley. It was Vikramjit's task, as Commandant of the CRP battalion stationed in Srinagar, to snuff out this invidious presence in cooperation with the local police. Contrary to common perception this was an extremely delicate task, requiring the skill and deftness of a brain surgeon maneuvering around the nerve centers to reach the cancerous cysts. But that was exactly why Vikramjit had been chosen to lead the battalion—he had the sensitivity and patience to deal with delicate situations.

The first year had been particularly tough, in what to them was a semi-alien environment. It felt as if their unit was ensconced in a wall-less fort surrounded by hostile forces they were powerless to control. And during that first winter they had to brave the bitter cold quartered in decrepit barracks on the outskirts of the city where the chill winds fought for entry into their living space. However, spring brought a thaw into their situation— both mental and physical. As happens quite often in life, the seeds of the change were sown quite by accident.

One morning Vikramjit had been travelling in his armoured jeep along the main highway leading out from the cantonment into the city. About fifty metres in front of him he could see a motorcyclist weaving erratically through the traffic of cars and scooter rickshaws that crawled along the road towards a triangular traffic island. As he watched he saw a woman, clad in a dark brown *phiran* and salwar, dashing across the street near the traffic island. She clutched the hand of a small child, almost dragging it along in her desperation to cross the road. What happened then was almost like a slow motion scene. The child heard the deep-throated roar of the motorcycle and froze in the middle of the road like a frightened foal, disengaging the mother's hand in the process. The motorcyclist darted out from behind a car, racing to overtake it. Before he realised it, he had knocked down the child. He hesitated a moment, then fled away from the scene. There was a screeching of tyres as all other traffic came to a halt. The mother had turned back, suddenly conscious that her child was not with her. She watched aghast at the little bundle of clothes lying in the middle of the road behind her and ran back to it shrieking in anguish. No one else stirred out of their vehicles, though a small group of passersby now clustered around the mother and child.

Vikramjit got out of his jeep, ignoring the protests of his two security jawans. He called to his driver to follow him after extricating the jeep from the queue of vehicles they were caught up in, and jogged his way towards the growing crowd chattering and gesticulating around the mother and child. Reaching the spot he jostled his way through the crowd till he reached the center. He saw that the child lying motionless on the road was a young girl of four or five years. Her mother sat on her haunches beside her, wailing and beating her head. As he approached the pair the noise from the crowd was reduced to a murmur, with an occasional voice whispering 'Commandant sahib'. Vikramjit asked for some water, and when someone brought it, sprinkled a little on the girl's face. She immediately opened her eyes and looked around in panic at the sea of faces peering down at her; then spotting her mother, whimpered 'Ammi' and clutched her hand.

Vikramjit could make out that the girl was suffering more from shock than any serious injury, but not wanting to take any chance he gently suggested to the mother that they take the girl to a doctor. The woman was too dazed to offer a reply. Vikramjit decided to take the initiative, and picking up the child asked the mother to follow him as he walked towards his jeep, which had by now drawn up near the spot. The child was examined at a nearby clinic and Vikramjit paid for the medical costs and gave a little extra to the mother for purchasing something nutritious for her daughter. Then he dropped them near the spot where the accident had taken place—where the mother had indicated their home was.

The event had a special impact upon Vikramjit. It was the first time that he had interacted with one of the 'locals'; not just the local officials and police officers, but with the common people. Brief though the interaction was, it uncovered for him the human face of the local population, which had hitherto been perceived as a faceless, hostile mass. He realised that there was no intrinsic difference between the pair and a similar pair that might exist in his native Bikaner in Rajasthan. Even the action of the unruly motorcyclist and the stream of car and scooter drivers who had only a callous curiosity to offer at the scene of the accident, could have been in Bikaner rather than here. It helped to dissolve the barrier of apprehension and distrust that had existed ever since he had come to the valley half a year back.

His altered perception also percolated to his battalion. News of his little action of concern and kindness spread slowly amongst his juniors and jawans. What was of added significance to them was the fact that their commandant could enter a crowd like that without any escort or protection and face not hostility but respect and admiration for his action. It brought to them the realisation that the enemy they had to fight—and be wary off—was not the common man but the handful of miscreants that had brought the State to its present state of turmoil.

The incident also brought about a change in the perception of the local people. Though there had been less than a hundred people who had witnessed the scene, the news of the incident had a ripple effect, with embellishments added at every subsequent stage. Srinagar was like a large village, at least in its laidback culture. By the evening a few thousand people had heard how the Commandant of the CRP battalion had leapt out of his armoured jeep, and picking up a child injured in a road accident, run all the way to the nearest hospital to save the child's life. And so it continued to grow and spread in the subsequent days.

The overall effect was that there was a significant mellowing of relations between the CRP and the people in the city—at least in the newer part of the city where the incident had taken place. The CRP jawans on routine patrol scowled less at passersby, sometimes even offering a tentative smile to the children; and the locals displayed less hostile suspicion towards the CRP jawans stationed at various pickets in the area, or patrolling the streets.

Vikramjit's interaction with the JKP was through an officer of about his own age, Rashid Ahmed, who had recently been promoted to the post of SSP. As per normal protocol the two forces had to collaborate actively to see that law and order was maintained in the city. Moreover, the intelligence wing of the JKP could provide vital inputs on the presence and movement of terrorists and local militant groups, and this was of crucial importance to both the agencies in performing their peace keeping task. In the few months that they had been interacting, the two officers had found that they shared a commonality of interests and attitudes that helped carry their relationship beyond the official to a personal level. On the morning of the accident, Vikramjit had been on his way to Rashid's office in the JKP headquarters. After dropping off the mother and daughter, Vikramjit had proceeded to his original destination.

"Well, well, well," Rashid had said as Vikramjit entered his office. "I believe you have been performing heroic deeds early in the morning."

"O, nothing yaar, I just helped out a young child involved in a road accident," Vikramjit responded. Then it dawned on him what Rashid had said and he asked, "But how do you know. I've just come straight from there?"

"Ah! That's the secret of our success," Rashid chuckled, "we don't just keep tabs on our enemies, but also our friends; and when a friend happens to be the CRP Commandant, well, wireless messages flash all over the city. But I have good news for you, which you can consider as the reward for your fearless deed. I have found some very good accommodation for you and your battalion right in the middle of the city. So no more roughing it out in barracks."

Sitting at the window, Vikramjit realized that he had now been enjoying this excellent view for well over two years. Under normal circumstances this would have been the time for him to receive orders for the battalion to move to a 'peace time' location, but Rashid had given him some exciting news a couple of months back, which he felt made it advisable for their unit to stay on for some more time. After extended confabulations, his HQ finally conveyed their acceptance of his suggestion for staying on in Srinagar for another year. The orders had reached him this afternoon and, therefore, he was able to relish his favorite scene even more this evening.

As he watched the sun dip over the mountains, he thought about the conversations he and Rashid had had over the past weeks, of how they could possibly proceed with their plans if he got his extension of stay. He must call up Rashid first thing tomorrow morning, he thought, and give him the news about his extension—and fix a time for them to meet and discuss further plans.

∞

"So the mandarins in the Home Ministry agreed with your HQ to let your battalion stay here for another year?" Rashid asked Vikramjit as they sat sipping coffee in Rashid's office.

"Yes," said Vikramjit, "but what is surprising is that they were able to take the decision in such a short period—just six-seven weeks. Normally those pen-pushers keep shuffling papers for months on end—till they have missed the train and the decision is already a *fait accompli*."

"Ah! But I didn't tell you," Rashid replied with a twinkle in his eye. "They did pass on the buck, by asking for a report on the situation from the State Home Ministry in Srinagar. This would effectively have delayed any decision by a few months. Our bureaucrats don't even know which end of the pen to write from, so they just forwarded the request on to the Police Department. And as Senior Superintendent Police for Srinagar it landed on my table. I immediately recognised from where this had originated and sent back a suitably positive report within twenty-four hours. So if the final decision took seven weeks to reach you, it just means that the bureaucrats at both ends couldn't warm their behinds with it for more than five-six weeks."

The both burst out laughing. Then Vikramjit said in a sober tone, "Now that this has been settled, let us not waste any further time. I know that you would not have sat idle in the meantime, so you should update me on the situation so that we can do some serious planning on the strategy we can use."

They were sitting in a little alcove in Rashid's office, where a sofa set made for less formal discussions away from his imposing desk. Rashid drained his cup and set it down on the centre table in front of him, then sitting forward on his sofa chair said, "As I told you some months back, our Intelligence Section had been picking up snippets of news about some sort of an informal survey being conducted by what appeared to be a civil liberties group. What aroused the interest of the Intelligence people was the fact that the questions being asked related to peoples' opinion about some of the less popular measures taken by individual separatist groups, which could be termed as infringing upon the citizen's rights for freedom. This was also why we thought that a civil liberties group was behind the move. Now the direction of these enquiries was extraordinary, since up till now no one had dared to question any of the *firmans*, or edicts of separatist groups, because these are normally backed by militants—whether imported terrorists or those of a local hue. Because of this unusual factor our Intelligence people continued probing the matter.

"Since I spoke to you a couple of weeks back, things have taken an even more curious turn. Initially these reports had been coming through separate agents and through diverse sources with diverse backgrounds. It seemed almost as if a professional consultancy organisation was conducting an opinion poll. But that is unheard of in the valley because of the inherent risk involved, especially when dealing with such delicate issues. No outside agency would take the risk of taking on such an assignment and no local agency exists that can undertake such a task. Then who? We intensified our investigations. And that is when we realised that what we had been following were strands of a single web. Slowly and methodically we followed the spokes of the web, advancing with every step closer to the centre—hopefully to where the spider resided." Rashid looked at Vikramjit with a smile before continuing. "We finally got a glimpse of the spider just a few days back."

"Well, who is it?" Vikramjit asked in irritation.

"It is a local businessman," Rashid responded, "who owns a handicrafts shop on Linking Road, but derives his importance from the fact that he has recently become the President of the Kashmir Chamber of Commerce."

"But that is hardly the profile of a revolutionary," Vikramjit said in controlled anger. "Is this what I have staked my career on, convincing my Headquarters about the possibility of 'the change in the air', the possibility of changes that could alter the course of history?"

"Hold your horses Vikramjit," Rashid interrupted hurriedly. "You are still not totally familiar with the culture of the people here to grasp what is happening. For one thing, I must inform you that it is not just this one man, it is his whole family who are involved: his wife and his son and his two grown up daughters. That means that what has been happening is at multiple levels; which is why we had been receiving inputs from different directions. Now what this implies is what you have to understand." He went on to explain how the different members of the family could influence diverse sections of society—ending with ". . . and last, but not the least, the wife. She grew up in the tranquility that prevailed here in this valley. She has seen the spectre of violence invading it. She is the stilled voice that has watched it all happening—and is now tired of it all. She wants a peaceful life—for herself, and for her children."

Vikramjit looked at Rashid in awe for a moment, then stood up and clapped. "You should have been a politician, or a poet, what are you doing in the police?"

Rashid looked at him a little sheepishly, waving to him to sit down, then said, "Alright, alright! I got carried away a little bit. But the core of what I was saying holds true. What we are witnessing is a new wave of an evolution in the embryo. It is in a very nascent stage, a very tentative stage, but it holds the potential for change. It is now up to us to see how we can protect it and nurture it."

"You really think that something can come out of this family affair?" Vikramjit asked, still not convinced.

"From what I can make out, these people are sincere and have decided that they would like to see a change. They are testing the waters to see how many others feel the same way before they commit themselves to action. From what inputs we have received so far, the feedback to their survey has been extremely positive. And this is positive for us as well. This is the sort of change that can counter the separatist thinking and enable a peaceful environment conducive to economic growth. But, as you implied, what can a family do. By themselves they would be very vulnerable to divisive forces, which would see in them an opponent—an enemy to their ambitions that needs to be eliminated. We will have to act as a shield to ward off such attacks. If we can be successful in our efforts, we will enable a growth of their movement—whenever they see the possibility of carrying it forward."

"Okay, I can see your point," Vikramjit said. "Even if there is one iota of a chance of their success, I am all for supporting it. But we must be careful that none of our actions can be construed to be supporting their movement; otherwise it will give the impression that this is a State sponsored movement. And that will give a weapon to others to discredit it, and this could lead to its failure."

"I agree with you entirely," Rashid concurred. "So let us see how things develop in the next few weeks, and then act accordingly."

"You do realise that my extension of stay is only for a year?" Vikramjit said.

"Don't worry," Rashid said. "If they can last out that long, they will be firmly entrenched to carry their plans forward; in which case I will just have to look for other support after you are gone."

On that note they parted—agreeing to meet frequently to monitor progress on the project.

A PROPOSAL AND A DEBATE

The Kashmir Chamber of Commerce had its office on the first floor of a building on the corner of Residency Road and Linking Road. Its meeting hall was big enough to accommodate about a hundred persons, with a low dais and a head table for speakers facing the audience. Normally, when only the office-bearers were meeting, a small conference room to one side was used; of course, the President, the Secretary and the Treasurer had their separate modest offices overlooking a small courtyard situated inside the complex. The fair-sized Reception area at the head of the entrance staircase was lined with portraits of some of the more prominent past Presidents. At the side of the door leading to the meeting hall was a brown wooden board with names of Presidents written sequentially in white paint, along with the years when they had held office. Just above Shafiq Ahmed's name was that of his predecessor Ramdev Chandra, who had held the Presidency for seven years. Shafiq Ahmed had now been in office for almost two years.

The meeting that day was one of their routine quarterly meetings and had been scheduled for twelve noon. Most of the members started dribbling in by eleven-thirty, rubbing their hands for warmth and calling out their greetings to those who had arrived earlier. A table with tea service had been laid out in one corner of the Reception area and as each new person came in he would head for it, collect his cup of beverage and biscuits, and join one or the other group of earlier entrants.

By ten to twelve the Reception area was packed with members and there was a long line of people awaiting their turn at the tea table. The early birds went through the open door of the meeting hall and congregated in small groups along the aisle near the east-facing windows, savouring the warmth of the sunlight streaming through them. There was a general hum of excitement as friends and acquaintances met and caught up with news about each other. As happened often at these periodic meetings at the Chamber, there was an atmosphere of disorderliness till fifteen minutes past the hour. Shafiq Ahmed and the Vice President of the KCC, Gulam Rasool, had arrived a few minutes before twelve, but waited till everyone had had their fill of tea and gossip before they called the meeting to order. It was wiser to have happy, contented members as an audience, especially when important, sensitive issues had to be discussed. For Shafiq Ahmed this was doubly vital, because there was one extremely sensitive issue he would have to put to vote towards the end of the meeting.

Finally, at twelve-thirty, Shafiq Ahmed tapped on the microphone in front of him to call the meeting to order. Along with him on the dais sat Gulam Rasool and three other senior members of the Chamber, Gulam Mohammed, Saleem Sheikh and Omar Sheikh, all in their late sixties, who Shafiq knew would support what he had to propose in connection with the second last item on the agenda, listed simply as 'Looking to the Future'. The meeting followed its normal course, with the Secretary presenting various points on the agenda and brief discussions on them by the members, or clarifications by the President or Vice-President. Just before one o'clock the penultimate point on the agenda was called out for discussion by the Secretary. There was a general murmur of speculation among the members about what this vaguely worded item could be about, and then everyone settled down to listen to what the President might have to say.

Shafiq Ahmed drew the microphone towards himself and cleared his throat. He looked around at the members sitting before him, gazing at him in anticipation. There were about fifty-sixty of them, which was an unusually high number for such a routine quarterly meeting. Most members were content to read the 'Minutes of the Meeting' when they were circulated a few weeks later. But Shafiq Ahmed had been active in the previous week, calling up members individually and requesting them to attend this meeting because there was something important to be discussed. Tapping softly with his finger on the microphone, more out of nervousness than to silence any conversations, he started.

"Friends, over the past few months I have met almost all of you individually, to share some of my thoughts and to elicit your opinion on certain extremely delicate issues that face us, as a business community, and as citizens of the valley. In case I have inadvertently missed out talking to some of you, I would like to apologise; but to make amends for my mistake I will re-state these issues now so that we are all cognisant of what we are going to discuss. Some of you might not agree with what I am about to say, but I request you to be patient and hear me out. After that there will be ample opportunity for everyone to express their views and debate the subject. Any decision that we might arrive on at the end of this meeting will have to have the consent of at least three-fourths of the members present.

"As we have all seen over the past two decades, the atmosphere in the valley has slowly changed, from one of peace and tranquility to that of increasing turmoil and violence. We have all felt this change in our daily lives, whether it be the effect it has had on our businesses, or on our personal lives and activities. Our businesses have been adversely affected by the increasing terrorist activities and the periodic hartals or strikes ordered by religious or political leaders. Tourists, who are the mainstay of commercial activity in the valley, are wary of coming here when there are frequent disruptions of peace. On a personal level, I have escaped financial ruin by sending my son and my salesmen to other parts of the country to sell our products. But how many of the shopkeepers can do that? And what about the hotels and houseboats and all those who cannot export their services—how do they survive? What about all those unseen faces, the makers of the handicrafts and garments and leather goods that we sell, how do they survive if we are not able to buy their products because our own sales are stagnant? In fact each one of us living in this valley is part of one large community whose life is dependent upon the other; if one part is sick that sickness seeps into the whole community—affects all of us in the valley. How long can we allow this situation to linger on?

"I talked about my son, who has joined me in my business; he goes all over the valley to purchase the products we sell, from the makers of handicrafts and people who weave and embroider. These are largely poor people who live in villages and small towns. What we buy from them is their main source of livelihood. The less we buy from them the less they have to feed their families.

"My daughters are studying in college. They have their own aspirations, their expectations from life. They have been outside the valley and seen what girls are doing—what they themselves could do. Back here they cannot even be sure they will be able to go to their college in the morning, because of the frequent hartals or cross-firing between terrorists and police, or random acts of hooliganism. Over the past year they have witnessed a gradual curtailment of their freedoms—whether it be the ban on music groups, or the edict by a fundamentalist group for all women to wear burqas when they step out of their houses. Cinema halls have all been burnt or shut, so there is no outside entertainment or extra-curricular activity they can look forward to. My daughters now tell me that they would like to study outside the valley where they can live a more free life; they feel stifled living here. My wife tells me that all the women in her neighbourhood feel the same. They are in a constant state of apprehension whether their husbands and children will come back home hale and hearty in the evening.

"I am quoting from the feelings in my own family because they probably mirror some of the feelings you also might be experiencing. What I have gathered from those of you to whom I have talked to about this earlier, you have similar feelings or experiences. So where do we go from here? What can we do to prevent this situation from deteriorating? Until now we have all been passive watchers, hoping that the government will do something. But everyone seems to be following a populist agenda. I feel that it is about time that we took the initiative to come out in the open and voice our opinion that we cannot have all these trumped up organizations—whether religious or demi-political—ruling our lives; that we are tired of a multiplicity of authorities governing our lives.

"Some of us have been talking to people in the villages and smaller towns all over the valley, and a majority of people have expressed the opinion that they agree with what I am saying; that they are sick of the way things have been going; that enough is enough! Everyone wants peace and prosperity, but someone has to take the lead to voice this opposition to the current state of affairs. Previously everyone felt that their voice would be heard through the duly elected governments; but the politicians have made a mockery of that exercise. However, there is a silver lining to that cloud: not all politicians are corrupt, or bad, or power hungry. There are still a few who have a genuine desire to meet the aspirations of the people. If we can reach a consensus on taking action today, we can approach such politicians and use them to bolster our case for promoting an environment that will be more congenial to peace.

"I know that this is not going to be easy, because the fundamentalists and the 'azaadi' brigade have become strong over the years; but unless we act now, we will only be allowing them to become even stronger—which will lead us all into ruin. I think that I need not say more, since I have already covered what I wanted to say. I now leave it to you to express your feelings about what I have said, so that we can arrive at some conclusion."

After Shafiq Ahmed stopped speaking there were a few moments of complete silence, then there was a clamour of voices shouting to be heard and many hands raised, expressing their desire to speak. Shafiq leant forward and motioned to a person in the third row to speak. Gulam Ali stood up and waited for everyone to become silent before he spoke. He looked all around him, then said, "Jenab President sahib, what you have said is true, but we cannot overlook another truth: the fact that the agitations that have been gaining ground in the past decade or more are based on the desire to be heard—for the voice of the Kashmiri people to be heard. People are frustrated, they are now impatient. We might be suffering in our commercial ventures, but that is a price we have to pay to gain our independence; a price that the present generation has to pay so that the next generation is free from this domination by the government in New Delhi."

There were a few voices shouting "Here, here!" and "Well said" as Gulam Ali sat down. It was the Vice-President, Gulam Rasool, who spoke up.

"Gulam Ali sahib, I would like to disagree with you. You talk of the 'voice of Kashmiri people'. I would like to ask, who are the Kashmiri people? Are these thousand, or two thousand, or even ten thousand people who join processions, or stone vehicles, or burn shops and houses, the Kashmiri people? Is this the voice that needs to be heard that you are talking of? Or is it the silent majority, which includes most of us here, and the large number of people that Shafiq Ahmed sahib talked about just now, who have so far sat back in impotent patience, whose voice needs to be heard? Let us not be so naïve as to deny the fact that these agitations, and the turmoil we have been facing all these years, is sponsored by Pakistan and has been brought to our doorsteps by terrorists sneaked across the border by them. Let us not be so naïve as to deny that it is Pakistani money that is funding the activities of these separatists and fundamentalist organizations. They are exploiting the weakness of our unemployed youth—an unemployment that has been mainly caused by these very agitations that are driving away the tourists from this valley."

Another member got up and shouted, "So what is wrong if Pakistan is doing this? They are only helping us to liberate ourselves from Indian rule. What is wrong if we want to join Pakistan?"

One of the senior members sitting at the head table, Omar Sheikh, raised his hand and said in a calm voice, "I would like to reply to our honourable, agitated member. Jenaab, I would like to draw your attention to what is happening to our erstwhile brothers across the border, in what is called 'Azad Kashmir'. They are azaad only in name, not even in the minds of their Pakistani masters who have called them that. They live in miserable conditions, in total subservience to the Pakistani army. What we used to call Kashmiriyat, the soul and culture of this valley, has been driven out of their minds and bodies;

at least we still retain a semblance of it here. A large part of it was drained out of our lives as well when we allowed our Kashmiri Pandit brothers to be driven out of the valley by these same terrorists and their lackey local collaborators. Let us wake up before we ourselves become victims of Pakistan's machinations. Let me assure you that they have no desire to liberate us; they only want to annex our valley and change it into another 'Azad Kashmir', which they can suppress and rule."

"But what is wrong if we want *azaadi*, our independence to rule ourselves? Before 1947 we were an independent State. Why can't we be like that again—without any Maharaja of course?" asked another member from the back row.

Omar Sheikh replied again, "There are two reasons for that not being possible. First, that both the Jammu and Ladakh regions will not accept that, and they are as much a part of the State of J&K as Kashmir is. If we were to accept that Kashmir could be an independent country by itself, we come to the second reason: how long would we be able to remain independent—to defend ourselves? You must remember that in 1947 it was Pakistan who sent across their forces in the guise of tribals to annex Kashmir; which forced the Maharaja to seek help from India to defend his State. Do you think they will not do so again if we are a small independent country?"

Shafiq Ahmed intervened saying, "I would like to add that what I am suggesting is that we try to re-establish the state we were in before this terrorism crept into the valley in the past two decades; that we try again to establish a more democratic state of administration with a more assertive voice from us who are the honest, hard working citizens with the largest stake in a peaceful environment. If we are more involved in the government instead of just watching and criticising it, we could weed out some of the corruption and make the government more accountable to us. And if we can give such a government the confidence to get rid of these divisive elements that are subverting our independence and basic rights, we would be able to restore peace and prosperity to the valley. I know this cannot be achieved overnight, that this will take time and a lot of patience, but don't you think it is worth the effort? And if you feel that it *is* worth the effort, I say that we have to make a start sometime—and that time is now!"

There was an instant burst of private discussions in the audience, in small groups and one to one; some whispered, some loud and heated. This continued for about ten minutes. Vice President Gulam Rasool had a whispered conversation with his companions on the dais, then rose and spoke through the microphone.

"Gentlemen, I have just spoken to my colleagues on the dais. We feel that the subject we have to vote on is serious enough for us to take a little more time to consider and to discuss among ourselves. At the same time it is serious enough for us to take a decision on it today. Because it is a part of the agenda for this meeting, we have to reach some decision before we conclude the meeting. In any case any delay would only mean an unwarranted procrastination. It has therefore been suggested that we disperse now for a short while. Tea and snacks are being laid out in the Reception. We will re-convene the meeting after an hour. Then we will put this proposition to vote. I hope that you agree with this idea."

There was a general murmur of assent and the members slowly started trickling out of the hall, still discussing the matter amongst themselves.

FOLLOW THROUGH

The ambulance sped along the river bank road towards Shri Maharaja Hari Singh Hospital in Karan Nagar, its siren blaring. Behind it a police jonga followed with its own shrill clarion call for all to clear the way. Inside the ambulance Bashir Ahmed sat holding his father's hand, mournfully watching the laboured rise and fall of his chest beneath the grey blanket that covered him. On the other side a medical attendant in white tunic and cap sat holding the stand from which the intravenous fluid dripped drop by slow drop into the tube that fed the life force into the patient's vein.

Bashir watched through the mist blurred ambulance window at the Jhelum flowing sluggishly below as they rushed past its placid waters. How could the river be so indifferent to the turbulence of life on its banks—so unmoved, so calm in the midst of all the turmoil? It had been like that ever since he could remember; the life-blood of the city which only threw its filth down its banks. Its calm flow taunted the impatience of those beyond its banks, watched disdainfully as they drew up intricate plans to change their worlds. How fragile is the skein of the web you weave—how fragile indeed your very lives, it thought. I am eternal and yet ever changing, the truth that you refuse to discern. Go, weave your webs, and let me go my way.

It had indeed been a hectic period for Bashir and his family—the past four years. At the same time it had been a period of excitement and exhilaration, as they struggled to draw up their plans and see them unfold into reality. Shafiq Ahmed's meeting at the Chamber, which concluded ultimately in endorsing his plans, was just the starting point; the marathon had still to be run. The drawings on the board still had to be converted, brick by brick, into the edifice that was only an ethereal vision in their minds.

Shafiq Ahmed and his friends in the Chamber started drawing out a list of the politicians they felt were equally anxious to restore peace to the valley; these were the people, irrespective of political affiliations, who were pragmatic enough to realize and accept the fact that India would never compromise its sovereignty over the State. Once that factor was removed from the equation it was a question of how to neutralize the foreign elements and their local supporters, who were the root cause of all the trouble. They knew that this would not be easy, but now that they were certain of a lot of support from people all over the valley, and from different rungs of society, they were willing to take the plunge.

The Chamber members were all well established business persons with a firm standing in the local society. Most of them also had friendly contacts with one or the other of the politicians on the select list they had drawn out. They divided the responsibility of who would contact whom amongst themselves. Within a few weeks all the politicians had been contacted and valuable feedback obtained on their reaction to the suggestions put forward by KCC. Though they all agreed that some effort should be made to bring about a turnaround in the conditions, there was a general skepticism on how this could be achieved. Quite a number of them were frank in admitting that they were apprehensive of the backlash they could face from the extremist groups that seemed to have such a stranglehold on large sections of the population.

The Chamber members had anticipated such a reaction and drawn out a plan of action that would be most acceptable to those with such reservations. The idea was to avoid any overt confrontation—to move instead on an issue that, on the face of it, appeared harmless and yet struck at the roots of what they meant to achieve. A few years back the Indian government had resurrected the idea of '*panchayati raj*', or devolution of power to councils of villagers for localized decision making and governance. Elections for such councils were stalled in Kashmir because of the militancy situation. What was suggested to the politicians now was that they move a resolution in the State Assembly to push forward the stalled plan to hold panchayat elections in villages all over the State. The politicians agreed that this was a measure liable to receive the least measure of resistance.

Six months down the line, after many a noisy scene in the Assembly, the resolution was passed. The main resistance had been on the point of how much autonomy and powers could be delegated to the panchayats, since this appeared to impinge upon the prestige and importance of the MLAs themselves. Shafiq Ahmed travelled down to Jammu in an effort to lobby with the members of the Jammu Chamber of Commerce and convince them to lend support to their cause. Fortunately, the JCC office bearers understood his underlying motive and agreed to push the MLAs from their region to support the move.

But getting the resolution passed was just the preliminary step. To get the administrative machinery rolling for the mechanics of holding the elections seemed to take endless time. In Kashmir valley particularly, security was a crucial factor to be looked into. Apart from local rivalries there was the looming threat of terrorist attacks; even the 'azaadi' brigade felt that any democratic exercise within the framework of the Indian constitution was a threat to their own movement since it undermined their ideology. Bashir and his sisters, and the large following of youth they had managed to win over to support their movement, played an important role in instilling enthusiasm among the villagers in seeing the process through to a relatively peaceful conclusion.

The JK Police, of course, had an equally large role to play in ensuring the successful culmination to the Panchayat polls. Rashid Ahmed had been closely following the growth of the movement spearheaded by Shafiq Ahmed and his family. In the initial year he, along with his friend and CRP counterpart Vikramjit Chauhan, had closely protected this core group surreptitiously. By the time Vikramjit's ultimate transfer drew near, the concept of the panchayat elections had come into focus. Rashid realized that he would have to seek support from the police network all over the valley, since his own jurisdiction was limited to the Srinagar range or district.

He took advantage of the next Zonal IGP meeting that was scheduled soon, when the SSPs from all fifteen Ranges in Kashmir came to Srinagar. On the sidelines of that meeting he shared his knowledge about the growth of this movement led by Shafiq Ahmed with his fellow SSPs, and impressed upon them the important role that the forthcoming panchayat elections were likely to play in the growth of the movement. All the SSPs agreed that they would put in an extra effort to ensure that everything proceeded without hitch.

The successful conclusion of the panchayat elections however, brought its own problems. The ISI bosses across the border realized the implications of this success. This was negating all their efforts to denigrate Indian dominance over the Kashmir valley. They instructed the terrorists sent into the valley to target the newly elected panchayat members and to shoot them or threaten them into resigning their newly acquired posts. They were able to achieve some level of success in the initial months, till the JKP swung into action and started providing additional protection in the villages. The success of the panchayat elections also had a positive outcome for the security situation. The villagers, who till then had docilely allowed the terrorists to seek refuge in the villages, or to launch their operations from there, now became more assertive and self-assured with the increased police presence in their midst. The terrorists soon found that the safe havens they had earlier relied upon were no longer secure for them. Encounters with the police increased and the numbers of the terrorists in the valley started dwindling slowly.

The success of the movement for establishing Panchayati Raj encouraged the Kashmiriyat Party (KP), as Shafiq Ahmed's group now called themselves, to take the next step in their effort to bring peace to the valley. The panchayats had been given a moderate level of autonomy and authority and financial support to undertake development projects within their limited spheres of influence. But this could, at best, achieve an uneven measure of success, dependent as it was on the efficiency and sincerity of the individual panchayats. What was required now was cohesion of the efforts of these two thousand odd panchayats so that some level of uniformity could be brought to the development. The upcoming State elections would provide this opportunity. The KP, with Shafiq Ahmed as its President, took the decision to field their candidates in all the constituencies in the valley. Their efforts in interacting with a large number of villages during the panchayat elections had already earned for them the gratitude and affection of a large number of people in the rural areas. The news of their success had also percolated into the urban areas. If they were now able to convert this into support for their candidates for the Assembly elections, they could well be on their way to gaining a position of power, from where they could complete their agenda of bringing peace to the valley.

The Kashmiriyat Party's foray into the arena of active politics was, however, not as smooth as they had expected it to be. When they had backed the Panchayat elections they were actually in the background: supporting a cause, an idea. They were not bothered whether candidates representing one particular party won or those of another—or even no party. They were simply supporting a democratic process. Here, when they were themselves one of the contestants in the field, they had to face the opposition of all the firmly entrenched parties. In addition, there was opposition from the separatists and the 'azaadi' brigade and other lumpen elements who were opposed to the very idea of an election under the Indian constitution.

Most of the MLAs who had supported them for the Panchayat elections had decided to switch their allegiance and join hands with the fledgling KP so that they could fully support that cause. The KP welcomed them into their fold because these were persons recognized for their honesty and dedication by the public, and, with their experience, would form a part of the group of candidates who stood a fair chance of winning their seats in the next Assembly. On the flip side, the KP faced a higher level of bitterness and ire from the parties these MLAs had deserted.

Once active campaigning started, a few weeks before the actual date of the elections, the full import of what they had committed themselves to dawned upon Shafiq Ahmed and his party colleagues. The fight was particularly acrimonious in the cities of Sopore and Anantnag where the terrorists and separatists had strong influences. Even in Srinagar, where most of the opposition parties and fundamentalist groups were headquartered, the antagonism to their movement was palpably stronger. However, as the party's objective and motivation slowly became clearer to the people, public opinion started swaying in favour of the KP and attendance at their public meetings started swelling. Their opponents—both democratic and non-democratic—who had earlier looked at them with a sense of condescension and derision, now discussed their growing popularity with worried frowns. While the democratic parties reacted by intensifying their campaigns sprinkled with false propaganda and vitriolic rhetoric, the undemocratic elements took recourse to sharpening their knives. The attack on Shafiq Ahmed that morning had obviously been the handiwork of the latter.

The ambulance lurched as the driver took a sharp turn to the left to get off the bund road onto the one leading to the S.M.H.S. Hospital. Bashir looked down anxiously at his father. The blanket had slide to one side with the sudden movement of the vehicle and Shafiq Ahmed's white *achkan*, with the two spots of spreading blood stains near his chest, were clearly visible. Bashir sighed deeply and looked impatiently through the windshield to see where they had reached. The buildings of the Hospital complex were just coming into sight.

∞

AIR WAVES

Sunil Vohra peeped into Roshan's cabin, a folded newspaper clutched in his hand. Roshan was going through some accounts worksheets he had just printed out from his computer, tallying the figures with notes he had on the notepad alongside him.

"Hey, Roshan!" Sunil called out softly from the doorway, "Do you have a few minutes to spare? I have something here that might be of interest to you."

Roshan waved him in, saying, "Come in, come in Sunil. Just sit down and give me a few minutes while I finish tallying these accounts. Then we can have coffee together while we chat. In fact why don't you ask Viru to get us the coffee while I finish this."

Sunil went out to hunt for the peon. He came back in a short while holding two steaming mugs and settled down in front of Roshan. "Couldn't find him," he murmured, "so I thought I might as well get it myself."

Roshan finished his scrutiny and put aside his papers. He reached across for his mug of coffee and smiled at Sunil, asking, "So what's this great news you want to share with me early in the morning?"

Sunil took a sip from his mug, then unfolded the newspaper he had placed on the table and asked, "Didn't you tell me that this friend you had in Srinagar was called Bashir Ahmed?"

"Yes, that's right," Roshan said, a puzzled look on his face. "What about him?"

"Well, coming through Raghunath Bazaar this morning," Sunil said, "I saw this copy of yesterday's edition of 'Kashmir Chronicle' lying among the assortment of newspapers outside the newsvendor's kiosk. Seeing the headline I got curious and read part of the report under it. Here, see for yourself." He slid the newspaper across the table towards Roshan.

Roshan leaned forward. The front page banner headline, in large letters, screamed:

LEADER OF KASHMIRIYAT PARTY SHOT!

"Funny," he mumbled, "that anyone should remember the concept of Kashmiriyat, and name their party on that in today's age of anarchy." Then he read the report under the headline:

Terrorism Returns to Central Srinagar

Yesterday saw the return of terrorism to central Srinagar after a long time. Jenab Shafiq Ahmed, a leading local businessman and President of the recently formed Kashmiriyat Party (KP), was gunned down by two motorcycle ridding youth at the corner of Residency Road and Linking Road at 11.30 yesterday morning. Shafiq Ahmed, who is also the President of the Kashmir Chamber of Commerce, had just come down after attending to his work at the KCC, and was talking with the Secretary of the Chamber on the pavement outside the entrance to the Chamber, when the two youth, who were obviously lying in wait, swerved across the intersection and pumped bullets into the duo. While the Secretary, Mr. Altaf Peer, escaped injury Jenab Shafiq Ahmed was hit on the chest. Seeing the President collapsing to the pavement, Altaf Peer ran down Linking Road to Shafiq Ahmed's shop, and called his son Rashid Ahmed.

In the meantime, two policemen who were patrolling the street saw the incident and called for help on their walkie-talkie. A police jeep arrived on the spot within minutes, and an ambulance soon after. Rashid Ahmed went along with his father in the ambulance to the SMHS Hospital. Latest reports from the Hospital state that Jenab Shafiq Ahmed is out of danger, though he is still in a critical condition.

The incident underscores the fact that though there has been no terrorist attack in this part of the city for over a year, that is no reason to lower the guard as far as security forces are concerned. It is quite obvious that the few terrorists that still remain holed up in the valley, are desperate to get whatever mileage they can get out of stray incidents like this one.

It may be mentioned that the decrease in terrorist attacks in the valley is largely due to the successful outcome of the Panchayat elections over a year back. With the rural areas no longer affording safe haven to terrorists, and the Indian Army's success in curtailing infiltration from across the border, terrorist activity in the valley is considerably reduced.

It would be pertinent to point out that it was the Kashmiriyat Party that was largely responsible for the move to hold the Panchayat elections in the State. Having crossed that hurdle, they decided to formally enter the political arena in these Assembly elections so that they could push forward their agenda. Since a number of sitting MLAs from established parties had supported them earlier, and since they strongly support the basic concept of the KP agenda, these MLAs have decided to join the KP and fight under their banner during the forthcoming elections. It is about time the JKP took the fledgling KP seriously and provide their leaders with increased security cover.

Roshan's eyes shifted to some smaller reports on the side, under the same banner headline. One read:

JKP Promises Enhanced Security

IGP Ali Sagar said in Srinagar today that the JKP would be enhancing security cover for all major political candidates standing for the Assembly elections. He admitted that their assessment of the threat perception to the fledgling KP candidates had been erroneous and they had not realized that this party had gained so much popularity in the short time they had been in the fray. This faulty assessment would now be rectified, Ali Sagar said.

SSP Srinagar Range, Rashid Ahmed, added that one of the shop keepers on Linking Road, who had witnessed the shooting, had had the presence of mind to note down the registration number of the motorcycle used in the attack. The witness added that though he had only had a fleeting glimpse, his impression was that the men on the bike were stockily built, and though the driver was clean shaven, the pillion rider, who had done the shooting, had a dark flowing beard. Details provided by the witness have been radioed to all JKP and CRP personnel and they hoped that they would soon be able to apprehend the culprits . . .

Another captioned report read:

Revival of Kashmiriyat

Bashir Ahmed, the son of Jenaab Shafiq Ahmed who was shot at on Linking Road yesterday, and who is the Secretary of the newly formed Kashmiriyat Party, assured this reporter that his father was now out of danger. Speaking outside the SMHS Hospital he said that, fortunately, the pistol used in the attack was of a small caliber, and that a large part of the impact of the two bullets that had hit his father on the chest had been absorbed by his thick layer of clothing, with the result that they had not penetrated very deep, and did not cause damage to any vital organ. These bullets had now been removed by the doctors. He said that the attack itself was traumatic for his father, who was a peace loving man, and he was now recovering from the shock. The doctors were confident that his condition would soon be stable.

On being asked by this reporter about the background for the naming of their party, Bashir Ahmed smiled and said in recollection, 'It happened a few years back during a discussion around our dining table at home. We were all disgusted and agitated about the way things were going. We wanted to do something about this, not just wait for someone else to rectify the situation. My sisters, who were in college, were the most vocal and indignant about the way things were. My mother, who had been listening to all this, started talking about how peaceful things had been before the terrorists started infiltrating into the valley. She talked about the unique culture of the valley where everyone lived in harmony and there was no space for religious fundamentalism. We, I and my two sisters, were totally enamored by the picture of tranquility that she drew for us with her words. That is what set us on the path that we are on now. So when it was finally decided that we form our own political party to fight in these Assembly elections, that picture of cultural harmony and tranquility, which my mother had talked about, came to mind. It was natural that we name our new party the Kashmiriyat Party. I know that there is some controversy about the origin and scope of the term 'Kashmiriyat', but the strongest message it conveys to the common man is that of the cultural ethos of the past that promotes peace and communal harmony. That is what we hope to achieve—Insha 'Allah.'

Roshan looked up from the newspaper he had been reading, a dazed look in his eyes.

"What happened?" Sunil asked. "Looks like you got a knockout punch. I've not read the full thing, but when I saw the name Bashir Ahmed I thought this just might be the friend you had mentioned once."

"Yes, it is the same," Roshan said softly, "even though from what he is quoted as saying, he seems to be a different person. He and Ravi were always quarreling about the status of Kashmir and Kashmiris, and here he is talking about Kashmiriyat—the cultural ethos of the valley and its non-communal traditions. I suppose twelve years is a long time, and people do change." He paused and looked unseeingly at the newspaper for a while, then said, "But I am being unfair. He was never communal in his thinking—just antagonistic towards Indians, because he thought they were the cause of all the trouble in the valley. He was always friendly and loyal to me and Ravi. In fact, I was recollecting the other day, he had promised to try and help me overcome my troubles the day before everything happened—the day of the fire. I never did get the chance to go back to meet him the next day as I had promised. So it was not he who could not live up to our friendship, it was I who couldn't make it."

"Forget it Roshan. You think too much, and you are too sensitive," Sunil said, trying to lighten his friend's mood.

"No, no," Roshan said, still looking down and lost in his thoughts. "But let me think. Should I . . .

For three days Roshan vacillated over what he should do. He had retained the cuttings from the newspaper Sunil had brought for him. Over the past days he had re-read them a number of times, pondering over the contents. There was a hint of optimism in what they conveyed—a ray of hope shining through the dark clouds. But there was also a foreboding: was there really a chance of change? And if there was, for whom? His life had already changed.

Why should the potential of change in that now far off valley hold any interest for him? And yet . . .

He felt an exhilaration, a thrill of excitement when he read the news clippings—as if there was something beckoning him, calling him to be part of a celebration. A vision of the meandering Jhelum floated in his mind's eye sometimes; sometimes the narrow lanes of Maisuma Bazar, or the stone facade of the Don Dosco School building. But then the flames from their house in Habba Kadal would engulf all other scenes and he would shudder out all other memories from his mind.

He had thought that the past was finally buried and done with—that he had opened a new chapter of his life. Now, it seemed as if someone had come and stoked a dying fire, prodded a heap of comatose ashes that covered a few smoldering embers, and an agonising heat glowed again beneath that heap and emitted the entrails of a dark grey plume of smoke that arose to choke him.

On the fourth day he decided to break out of his apathy and confront his emotions. What did he want? Why was his mind suddenly in turmoil? Why should those little snippets of news disturb his peace so much? He finally broke through the barrier of his vacillating mind and approached the Telecom office in Jammu. Could they please give him the contact number for Ahmed Joy & Sons, Linking Road, Srinagar?

Later, punching the number on his phone in office, he held his breath for a while. The telephone on the other end rang for a long while before someone picked it up. "Ahmed Joy & Sons!" a person almost shouted into the phone. Roshan smiled to himself, imagining that the person on the other end had been sunning himself in front of the shop, and had run in when he finally heard the phone ringing. It truly reflected the lackadaisical pace of life in Srinagar. Obviously things had not changed very much over the years. "Hello! Hello!" the voice shouted impatiently from the other end.

"Hello," Roshan finally responded. "Could I speak to Bashir Ahmed please?"

"Bashir sahib not here. Who is speaking?"

"My name is Roshan, Roshan Bhan from Jammu. When can I speak to him?"

"I cannot say," the person said peremptorily. "If you give your number I can give to him. He can call you if it is important."

Roshan gave him his mobile number, not knowing when Bashir would be able to call back, if at all. Then he got busy with his work, wondering whether he had done the right thing in calling up Bashir. What would he say if Bashir did call back? What could he do? How would he explain his silence over all these years—his lack of effort to get in touch? Well, anyway, he had made the effort now and the deed was done. Let's see what happens. At least he had got it off his mind.

Bashir rang up less than fifteen minutes later, his voice excited, "Roshan? Is that Roshan Bhan? Where are you?"

Roshan smiled with happiness hearing the excitement in Bashir's voice and said, "Yes, this is Roshan Bhan, your friend. I am speaking from Jammu."

"Friend, what friend?" Bashir replied in mock resentment. "You did not even care to get in touch in all these years. You are as bad as Ravi."

"What do you mean?" Roshan asked in surprise. "Ravi is not in Srinagar? Where is he?"

"Of course Ravi is not in Srinagar," Bashir replied. "He disappeared soon after you did. He went away for studies to the USA. And then took a job there. He did not bother to contact me either in all these years. But what a coincidence, he rang up yesterday from America. We had a long chat over the phone. He said that he had heard about my father being shot at and wanted to know if everything was alright. I told him that everything was okay now, and that my father was going to be discharged from hospital this evening. Anyway, Ravi asked how things were otherwise—whether life was normal and whether it was safe to visit. I told him that life was almost normal here and it appeared that the shooting at my father was most probably due to political rivalry rather than the act of a terrorist; at least that is what the police think now. You know, we have launched a new political party of our own. It is getting very popular, and that is what probably prompted the attack on my father from one of the other parties."

"Yes, yes," Roshan interrupted impatiently. "I read about your Kashmiriyat Party in the newspaper that reported the shooting at your father some days back. But is it true what you said to that reporter—that your party wanted to revive the concept of kashmiriyat in the valley? Are you sure that you are not saying all this for getting political mileage: to fool the people into voting for you, like all the other parties do?"

"No Roshan, I swear that we are sincere in our motives. We genuinely want that change to come about—and so do a lot of other people here. Everyone is sick and tired of all this terrorism and the stupidity that the fundamentalists are spreading. Even though we had to form a political party to fight the elections, people recognize that we truly represent their aspirations and are the best hope for bringing about peace in the valley. They are willing to give us a chance. So let us see."

"But what happened about your anti-Indian feelings?" Roshan asked almost in a teasing tone.

Bashir replied with a sigh, "I suppose a lot of us have reconciled ourselves to the fact that India will never let go. So what we are doing is just prolonging our agony by dreaming impossible dreams. But more than that, we have begun to realize that acceptance of the present arrangement is our best option. What KP's motive is, is to trade least resistance for least interference from the Center. But why are we discussing all this over the phone? Why don't you come over and see for yourself—feel for yourself? You might even be able to help us out in our efforts for achieving the change we are trying to bring about."

"Are you mad?" Roshan retorted. "You think I would be willing to take the risk of doing that after all that has happened in the past?"

"No, I am not mad," Bashir responded in a gentle tone. "I would never urge you to do anything that would put you at unnecessary risk. I can assure you that there will be as little risk to your person as there is to me and my family."

"You can say that after what happened to your father?" Roshan asked with a half laugh.

"I know, that was bad. But security has now been tightened for all of us, and more than that we have ourselves become more conscious about not exposing ourselves to unnecessary risks. In any case the attack on Abba was because of his political status. The same does not apply for everyone," Bashir said with seriousness. "But I have deliberately kept the clincher till the last. Ravi is coming!"

"What!" Roshan shouted into the phone, getting up from his chair in his office.

"Yes," Bashir laughed. "I knew that would shake you. I told you earlier that he had called from America. He said that he would like to come for a couple of weeks if it was safe. I told him the same thing as I did to you just now. So he agreed to come in a week's time and stay for two-three weeks, then spend the rest of his vacation with his family in Delhi. He will be staying at their Shivpura house, which will be cleaned up and made ready for him by the servants who are still there. I am sure that he would love to have you staying with him, if you agree to come. He is going to call me up and inform me about his flight details in two-three days, so tell me of your decision by then, so that I can convey it to him."

Roshan thought for a while. No, he could not go; it would just revive those unpleasant memories of his last days in Srinagar. But, it could also refresh all those pleasant memories of his childhood that kept on popping up in his mind from time to time—that kept on preventing him from burying the past and living his new present. And if Ravi was coming . . .

He finally said to Bashir in a hesitant voice, "Let me think this over. You realize how tough it is for me? I'll call you back tomorrow. I suppose you have called up on your mobile, so I can call you directly at any time."

And, on that note, they rang off.

ELECTION TIME

By the time Ravi and Roshan landed up in Srinagar, elections were just ten days away. There was a feverish air of anticipation in the air; a hope for change tinged with the hopelessness of unfulfilled promises that had gone before in the decades of such exercises that had preceded this one. And yet, the Kashmiriyat Party had gained a ground swell of support from the common people who were gasping for change—a breaking of the shackles that imprisoned them with the populist maneuvers of the earlier established parties. People were sick of the corruption that had become the epitome of those parties. They were wary of their regurgitated promises. They wanted peace; they wanted a tranquility that would allow them to live their lives without terrorist threats and the stranglehold of the fundamentalists.

Who ruled them had no meaning for them—as long as they got the freedom to live their lives without fear. What was India, what was Pakistan, what was 'azaadi' had little meaning for them if it did not allow them their peace of mind. The Kashmiriyat Party promised that and they were prepared to try out this new experiment. Perhaps it would work? Perhaps they could be left alone again, to till their lands and to labour for their living and enjoy the fruits of their labour without the thugs that sucked their lifeblood to feed themselves and their masters: the numerous warlords that now proliferated in the valley like wild mushrooms. Perhaps? One last throw of the dice? They had nothing to lose. Had they not already lost all?

Ravi and Roshan stayed at the Shivpura house, away from all the turmoil, but they were inexorably sucked into it because, after all, they had come for Bashir. Bashir, as the Secretary of the KP was the fulcrum on which the fortunes of the party turned. His father was still recovering from his wounds, so the burden fell that much more on him and his sisters. Salima was very much in the fray since she was standing from the Habba Kadal constituency, but Sabah was equally embroiled in the organizational work along with her brother. Bashir wanted his friends to help him out with his party work. They were reticent at first, then gave in thinking that they might as well put in their weight if it could help the KP cause in any small way.

Salima pleaded with Roshan to help her in her constituency. Roshan shied away from it. The very thought of visiting the area filled him with dread. Then slowly he acquiesced—perhaps this would be the way to exorcise the dread of the tragedy that had befallen their family. Perhaps restoring some element of equanimity would bring peace to his sister's soul? The first time he visited the area again, Ravi and Bashir decided to accompany him. They realized that it would be a traumatic experience for him and wanted to lend support to him. They all went to the site of Roshan's house. The burnt out skeleton of the structure still stood as it had over the past decade—as if no one dared to desecrate the site of that sacrificial act. Roshan broke down as he entered the grounds, kneeling amongst the cold, windswept ashes. His friends stood beside him, sharing his grief. After some time, Roshan wiped the tears from his face and asked for an urn. He collected some ashes and filled the earthenware pot that was brought. Ashes were ashes; whose, what, where, it did not matter. What mattered was the act. He would spray them in the Jhelum and liberate Rohini's agonized soul. Let the river's currents carry away the dank memories along its turbulent currents to the calm ocean, to mingle with the salt that nurtured the earth.

Ravi was constantly with Sabah, helping her in whatever way he could in the administrative work she had to do to support the Party's candidates in different parts of the valley. They travelled frequently to the outside constituencies, attending rallies and public meetings. Sabah was shy by nature, not the firebrand that her elder sister was. She preferred to stay out of the limelight—provide moral support and advice that the candidates and party workers required. And since the foundation of the party was laid upon the ordinary men and women who had little political experience, her quiet strength was just the elixir that gave the necessary impetus to them to carry forward the battle.

This suited Ravi, because he too had no desire to be in the forefront of any public exposure; but he was deeply impressed by Sabah's determination and strength of character. With every passing day he was drawn closer to her. Towards the end of the day, as they travelled back to the KP office, they could relax after the tension of the day's hectic activity and chat about their likes and dislikes and their lives and ambitions. After the first couple of days of reticent, reserved, formal chit-chat, their conversations became more exploratory, more intimate. By the end of the week they had become friends who could almost share their innermost thoughts and desires. The bonds that brought them closer and intertwined their thoughts washed away the differences in their ways of life and cultures; bonds that were human, superseding their difference of religion and upbringing.

It was the last day of campaigning—two days before the electorate went to vote. Ravi had accompanied Sabah to Bijbehara, just beyond Awantipur, where she had to attend a public meeting to provide the last boost to the local candidate's campaign. The meeting ended at around 4.30 p.m., but then there was a small farewell tea party where a number of prominent local citizens were invited. Farooq Sheikh, the KP candidate for that area pleaded that Sabah stay on till the party ended, saying her presence would enhance his stature among the guests and bolster his chances of winning the seat. They finally left an hour later, apologizing that they needed to reach Srinagar before dark.

A short while later, crossing the plateau where the saffron fields stretched to the horizon, Ravi said nostalgically, "You know Sabah, twelve years back Roshan and your brother and I were crossing this plateau and admiring the view of the saffron fields and the range of snow-capped mountains on the horizon. It was early morning and there was mist in the air and the sun was just a dull golden ball trying to pierce the mist. We had finished our final exams at school a few weeks earlier and had decided to go on a short trek beyond Pahalgam. It was a lovely time, and we were at a lovely age, where all the troubles and travails of life had still not overtaken our lives. It was fun being together for those few days with no cares to cloud our lives." Ravi lapsed into silence for a brief while, then sighed and said, ". . . as the poet said, 'what a tangled web we weave . . .'." He watched the crimson glow of the sun as it started its descent beyond the mountain range.

Sabah looked towards the same dying glow and said in a soft, sad voice, "And in a few days you will be gone again—to untangle some webs in Boston?"

"No Sabah," Ravi said, "the webs that were woven here were frightening enough to drive us away—Roshan and me and thousands of others. It is good to see that you are trying to untangle them and free yourselves from them."

"And you? Will they not free you too, so that you can come back?"

"I doubt it Sabah. You see, it is like the drops of water in the stream—in the Jhelum. Once they have floated past the bridge, they do not come back; they carry on their journey with the stream."

"But they do come back sometimes," Sabah said, turning towards him. "They do come back sometimes as raindrops, to rejoin the stream and restart their journey from under the bridge."

"Yes," Ravi said, smiling at her, "but that is as a reincarnation. Maybe . . . maybe the soul is the same, restless to re-visit its previous unrequited desires; but the previous drop has to complete its journey all the way to the ocean before it can sublimate itself into the blue heaven and assume the new entity."

"I never realized that you are a philosopher—a poet," Sabah said, a mischievous glint in her eyes. "Has anyone told you that before?"

"Yes," Ravi said with a chuckle. "Roshan. He used to tease me about that just after we had joined college. He used to say that I should have taken English Literature as a subject instead of Economics; then I could have become the 'Sheikh Peer' of the valley."

They both burst out laughing, then Sabah said, "That's a good one, though not all that original. I've heard that before from someone in college. But tell me, why are you in Boston now and working as an executive? From what I heard from Bashir, your father is rich and wanted you to come back and start a new business, or an industry."

"Was," Ravi said in a serious tone, "he was a rich man before all these troubles started here and he had to eventually leave in a hurry, leaving his business to be looked after by some of his employees. He did come back a few years later, but realized that his employees had embezzled a lot of funds. In any case all his previous contacts, his agencies, had dried up, so he just sold off the shop and business at whatever low rate he could get. He had no desire left to carry on here, even though he retained the house in Shivpura where I am staying now. He is still a rich man, but does not have the will to start a new business. He keeps asking me to come back, but I like the life I have made for myself there in Boston. I have a house on the edge of a hilly forest in the suburbs, away from the scramble of the busy city. Sometimes I look out of the window and see the maple leaves change colour from green to yellow to red and rust. Then I think of the chinars here in the fall and dream that I am back."

"So you do feel lonely sometimes, living all alone in your house at the edge of the forest," Sabah said, looking at him through the corner of her eye. "Why didn't you get married? You must be almost thirty now—same as my brother."

They lapsed into silence as Ravi lost himself in his thoughts. Then he said with a dreamy half-laugh, "Perhaps because I never met anyone like you . . . ?"

Sabah looked at him, startled. He was looking out of the other window. She blushed and turned her gaze away. They were just entering the city, and would soon be back at her house, where he had to drop her.

That night she dreamt of a wooden slope-roofed house in the middle of a forest. It was night and she was looking out of the window at the maple trees shedding their leaves. They are so much like the *chinars* in Kashmir, she thought. A brown carpet of dying leaves covered the ground and rustled with the soft breeze that brushed through the garden. As she watched, a white rabbit hopped out from behind a rock, scampering through the fallen leaves in the silvery moonlight. She tried to reach out to touch it, to stroke its soft fur and cuddle its warmth, but Ravi held back her hand and whispered softly in her ear from behind, "Let it go, let it run free to live its own life . . ."

TIME TO BID ADIEU

Roshan had left two days back—the day after the campaigning for the election had ended. Bashir and Ravi had pleaded with him to stay on another week till the results of the polling started coming out, but he would not be persuaded. His excuse was that he did not have any leave left, but they could feel that he was exhausted—struggling to break loose from the yoke of duty he had borne for the previous ten days. He had undertaken the task of helping Salima to campaign for her election from the Habba Kadal constituency, but every evening, when he returned to the Shivpura house, Ravi could see that he was emotionally drained by the task. He went through with it because he believed in what Bashir's party was trying to achieve, and because of his friendship and loyalty for Bashir, but ultimately, it was also as a sort of atonement for what had happened to his sister.

Sometimes, as he and Ravi sat on the lawn after dinner, Ravi could feel his friend's agony and emotional exhaustion from his day's efforts. Ravi would try to dissuade him from going through the experience again the following day, but Roshan was adamant. Now that he had started on this journey he wanted to drain himself till the last drop of energy remained within him—a sort of catharsis of his soul. Ravi gave up his efforts; he could only stand back and watch in sympathy and pain. Perhaps it was better that Roshan go through this self inflicted penance.

On the day before Roshan was to leave, with the frenzy of campaigning finally over, the three friends decided to spend the evening together, just by themselves. After a relaxed morning and lunch, Ravi and Roshan walked up the narrow lane from their house to the fork where it met the broader road near the Bund. With time on their hands they decided to continue along the Bund for the kilometer long walk to Linking Road.

Even though they had spent their nights and mornings in the same house for the previous ten days, they had not had the opportunity for any leisurely talks, because of the hectic schedule they were following. Now, for the first time, they were relaxed and could exchange notes about how they had lived their lives in the decade and more that they had been out of touch. As they strolled along the Bund, watching the Jhelum flowing serenely below them, Roshan recounted the struggle he and his family had been through after the holocaust; the trauma of their lives as refugees in the camp in Jammu, and how they had slowly crawled out of that dark phase to re-start their lives and live again as normal human beings. It had been a tough time, and many a time they had almost given up the effort to hold on to the slender thread that kept them alive. But, ultimately, life still had to be lived; their destinies still had to be fulfilled, as God had ordained.

Roshan finally sighed, then said, "But now all is well, as well as it can be. I have a good job, as Head Accountant at this research institute in Jammu. My parents have aged prematurely with the loss of their daughter and the loss of their homeland. But they have also learnt to accept this new life—though the summer heat in Jammu is like living in Hell. And then we dream of being back in our beloved Kashmir."

"Do you think you could come back here?" Ravi asked, "if this experiment of Bashir's party is successful, if things return to normal here?"

"I don't know," Roshan replied pensively, "I don't think so. How can one forget the wounds inflicted in the past? How can one live with constant apprehension of what could happen the next day? How can one live looking constantly over one's shoulder, awaiting another treacherous attack? Once the paradise is lost, it is better to come down and live on earth, wherever that might be." He paused, lost in thought, then shrugging off his mood asked, "But what about you? You have not said anything about your life for all these years."

"I'm afraid there is not much to say," Ravi replied. "I left soon after you did. With you gone, and all the troubles brewing here, I had no desire or motivation to study here. I just could not concentrate, so I discussed it with my father and we decided that I go to USA and do my graduation from there, and my MBA. Well, I just stayed on and found a job, which I like. So that's it. I do sometimes think of our life here when we were young, growing up. But that was another era, another phase of our lives. One can be nostalgic about it, but one cannot relive it. It is all water under the bridge—flowing around the bend and lost to sight."

They walked on silently for some time, lost in their own thoughts till they crossed Mahatas Studio and went down the stairs to Linking Road to meet Bashir. Bashir was waiting for them and they set out immediately for their little excursion to resurrect a part of their past. For a start, they stopped at Shakti Sweets on Residency Road and found themselves a table near the glass fronted entrance. They ordered tea and *samosas* and waited excitedly for the piping hot fare to arrive.

"So? What next?" Ravi asked, looking at Bashir.

"Maybe some kebabs at Adhoos?" Bashir said, deliberately pretending not to understand the implication of Ravi's query. "O, but I forgot that you are a vegetable," he said in mock remembrance.

They all burst out laughing. Then Roshan said with a mischievous glint in his eyes, "Remember Pahalgam—and what I told you about the multi-purpose ladle?" And they burst out in another fit of laughter as they watched the tea and *samosas* being placed in front of them.

"But seriously Bashir," Ravi asked again, "if your party gets some sort of decisive say in affairs after the election results come out, what do you plan to do about it? It is alright to ride high on a popularity wave, it is another thing to sustain that momentum of support unless you convert your promises into reality."

"I know Ravi. We are conscious of the fact that the expectations of our supporters will be at a high level. We realize that a lot of the previous resentment and belligerence among the youth will still be on the boil. So our first step will have to be to see how we can harness that energy and channel it into productive and constructive activity. Lack of employment opportunities has been one of the major reasons for unrest in the past, so that is something we have to look into as being one of our immediate areas of focus."

"Yes, that is true," Ravi said, dipping his *samosa* into the plate of chutney sauce. "Well, tourism will pick up next season once word gets around that things are returning to normal, but that will not be sufficient to absorb the huge mass of unemployment. What you need is industrial growth, and that is not something that will happen overnight. Industrialists, businessmen, they need to see sustained normalcy over a period of time before they will risk their money in any venture here."

"Value addition, that is what we want to try and promote as a first step," Bashir said. "So many fruits and nuts and other natural products are being exported out of the valley now; what we can do is . . ."

They continued with their discussion till they had finished their snacks. Then they crossed the street and climbed the stairs onto the Bund talking of various things. Strolling along for some time they found one of their previous favourite spots on the low parapet wall on the Bund and sat there facing the river their legs dangling over the side. They chatted for a long time, recollecting episodes from their days in school—events that at that time had seemed so momentous but now, in retrospect, evoked mirth. Then, with the sun losing its warmth, it was time to leave.

"So Roshan," Bashir asked, "any chance of your moving back here? You know that that is one of the salient points on our election manifesto—to create conditions whereby the Pandits can come back and we can again be one big family."

"Yes," Roshan said solemnly, "I have read your manifesto a number of times over the past days, but that is easier said than done. It is difficult for people here to realize the trauma our community went through during that period—both here and subsequently with our so-called rehabilitation. The scars, the scabs still remain to serve as reminders. It was a crisis of faith—not just from here, but also from where we were dumped. We have just crawled back to normalcy; I doubt that any of us would be brave enough to take another plunge so soon. I am truly happy that you are trying so hard to turn things around. I sincerely hope that you will be successful in your efforts. Maybe a new generation will emerge from amongst us that will venture forth and come here to help you realize your dream."

Bashir did not say anything; he just hugged Roshan tightly, letting his love for him flow through that embrace, as he bid a silent farewell to him and then walked quietly down the steps from the Bund towards his shop. Roshan and Ravi walked along the Bund towards their house, sightlessly watching the river flow by.

❧

Ravi stayed on another week, but Roshan's departure had left a vacuum in his life—a depression that was difficult to overcome. He had, for the first time, felt the depth of the Pandit community's plight from what Roshan had said on that final day. He realized what the difference could be between what one read perfunctorily in newspaper reports and what the experience could be like for those who were the actual protagonists in the tragedy that had been enacted.

To free himself from his bouts of depression he would walk along the Bund, sometimes all the way to Amira Kadal. One day he decided to go and see their old house in Wazir Bagh, where all his childhood had been spent. The house looked decrepit and deserted. A couple of windows on the second floor, in what had been his room, were half open and hanging loose on single hinges. There were a few stripped cotton underwear drawers fluttering from the window sills, obviously laid out to dry. As he stood there, gazing up at his erstwhile home, a disembodied voice ordered him to move on. He realized that there was a camouflaged sentry box jutting above the boundary wall on one side. The voice had obviously come from inside its dark interior.

As he moved further along the road he saw that the next building had a board in front of it proclaiming it to be the Head Quarters of a CRP Battalion. On making enquiries he was informed that both buildings had been leased out to the CRP a long time back. Their erstwhile house was now being used by the battalion jawans. His depression deepened and he turned back the way he had come, in no mood to proceed towards A.S. College as he had earlier planned.

On most days, after his strolls down memory lane, he would end up at the KP office on Residency Road by mid-afternoon. Sabah was always there, catching up on the Party work that had been neglected because of the election fever. Ravi invariably persuaded her to accompany him to the coffee house nearby, or go for a short stroll along the Bund. They talked about various things that affected their lives, or subjects of common interest.

With two days left for Ravi's departure, he asked Sabah to come out for what would be their last chance to go out alone, since the next day counting of votes was to start. They were strolling along the Bund when Ravi said, "Sabah, a long time ago, just before Roshan and Bashir and I had completed school, we were sitting here discussing our future plans. Your brother mentioned that he might not attend college because his father wanted him to join their business. I tried to convince him that going through college would broaden his perspective on life if nothing else. I remember that I told him that there was a whole new world that he would be missing out on if he joined the business at such a young age. Well, what happened subsequently is another matter, and he has done quite well for himself, but don't you feel that just being cooped up in the valley life is constricting—that one could gain a much wider perspective on life if one were to travel, or to go out of the valley for further studies, or take a job elsewhere to experience a different environment? Don't you sometimes feel that Srinagar is such a village, such a closed society?"

Sabah thought for a little while, then said, "You are right of course Ravi, Srinagar is such a small village in its temperament and outlook. When the fundamentalists were gradually tightening the noose with their ever more throttling *firmans*, it was becoming like a prison. That is when we rebelled—started fighting back. Let us see how the election results shape out. If we get some sort of say in decision making we will definitely try to break free of these strangleholds."

"But you will still be in a village," Ravi insisted, "perhaps a large village with a population of a million plus, but still a village in its thinking and outlook."

"And what's so wrong in living in this village?" Sabah said, smiling to take the edge off the aggression that her question implied. "It is a pretty village in a heavenly environment."

"Yes, but in a decade from now, with increasing population and pollution and industrialization coming in, it will change. Then it might be too late for you to escape." He thought for a moment and said with a tinge of bitterness, looking down at the river, "But I suppose that you will be happily married to a prosperous businessman by then, and have a brood of children to look after."

Sabah looked at him with a sidelong glance, a hint of a bemused smile upon her lips, and asked, "Do you have an alternative to offer me?"

Ravi said with a woeful sigh, "I wish I had."

They were both silent for a long time, but beneath that silence was an intuitive understanding of what the other one was thinking. However there were still a few gossamer threads of resistance that formed a fragile barrier that prevented them from speaking out the innermost thought and desire that lurked in their hearts.

The plane lifted off the runway with a triumphant roar, then calmed itself to an even rumbling grumble as it soared over the sprawling city and floated in a gentle arc to face back towards the south of the valley, arching steeply up to reach for the dazzling blue sky. Ravi pressed his head against the plexiglas to watch the matchbox houses give way to the patchwork of fields interspersed with groves of neatly marshaled trees in the fruit orchards. Somewhere in the distance the Jhelum swayed like a silver ribbon in a gentle breeze, among the green-brown tapestry. Soon the long range of snow-capped mountain peaks appeared to his right, sparkling white in glinting glory as they sailed past his window. All too soon the valley was left behind, and he gazed with unseeing eyes as they glided silently over the puny barren mountain ranges dwindling towards the plains.

Lost in thought Ravi marveled at the magic of the passage of time. Just over two weeks back he had been heading in the opposite direction, full of anticipation of what lay ahead: meeting his friends, reliving memories, dusting off the cobwebs that had clouded the past—and, at the same time, with a cautious hope of witnessing the unfolding of the changes that Bashir had talked about over the phone. And, once he had landed, the experience had been like a mixture of a gushing mountain stream and a placid lake surface; a mixture of the frenetic pace of the election campaign and the quiet talks they managed to squeeze in whenever the opportunity presented itself.

He was happy to have had the opportunity to stay again at the Shivpura house. It had a leisurely atmosphere that he had not remembered from earlier. His father had designed it like a large Swiss chalet, surrounded by a garden on one side and fruit orchards all around. It, however, held no ghosts for him since he had lived there only briefly before he went away. His visit to the Wazir Bagh house had been a numbing shock. That was the house that had held a horde of memories. However, it stood now like a forlorn, desolate carcass of its former pulsating self, waiting to crumble and die.

There were so many other memories that he had been able to revive in those last few days—some happy, some sad. What he was unable to shrug off even now was the memory of what Roshan had related and said on the last day before he had left. Ravi constantly felt a stabbing pain of doubt and guilt—could he have prevented it? But what was the use now, regrets would not erase what had already transpired. As he had thought that time, gazing through the bedroom window of his house in Boston, God did not take sides, He stood impervious to the little machinations of puny man. So whether it was Ravi's fault in not reporting the presence of the ominous strangers in Aru, or his failure to warn Roshan about the impending disaster in Srinagar, it was a flow that was pre-ordained. All water under the bridge—as he was so wont to saying.

His thoughts changed tracks, and a faint smile spread across his face as he looked at the warm sky outside the airplane window. Yesterday had been good. He had got up with the knowledge that the counting of votes would start that morning, and by that evening they would have a fair idea of what fate lay in store for the KP. He knew that Sabah would be stationed at the KP office on Residency Road, and he looked forward to meeting her again—perhaps for the last time. Bashir and Salima planned to remain at the counting centre, feeding Sabah with information on their mobile phones.

Ravi got ready and had a leisurely breakfast before he started off on his now routine walk along the Bund to the city centre. The sun's rays shone obliquely, peeping over the trees on the far shore to light up the little ripples on the river as it swerved around the last bend before it headed towards Zero Bridge. Everything seemed to be brimming with excitement over the anticipation of the coming events; or was it just his own mood transposing itself on his surroundings?

When he reached the KP office a number of Party workers were already there, dusting off the tables and sprucing up the 'scoreboard'—where the election results would be put up and updated as they came in. Sabah stood at the window on the far end of the room, near where the 'scoreboard' was. She seemed to be lost in thought as she gazed out of the window. Ravi walked slowly across the room and stood beside her and asked, "So, D-Day?"

Sabah half turned towards him, though still looking out of the window and said, "Yes, I suppose so. We will know soon enough how sincere people were when they said they supported our cause." She paused, then said in a soft voice, "So you are off tomorrow, back to your 'whole new world'?"

Ravi thought that he detected a note of mild bitterness, or was it concealed regret, when she said that, but chose not to register it. Instead he said in an even tone, "Yes, after I visit my parents in Delhi I have to get back to work."

Sabah was silent for some time, then asked, "What's it like in Boston, Ravi? Are there good colleges there? Many foreign students?"

"O yes," Ravi answered enthusiastically, "some of the best colleges in the US—in the world I would say. And yes, there are quite a few foreign students, even Indians. Why, are you interested? I could send you detailed information and brochures on some of them if you like. If you could get into Harvard for a post-graduate course there is nothing like it."

Sabah was silent for some time, still gazing out of the window. Then she said in a subdued voice, "I am a little frightened of your 'whole new world'. Of course there is first the question of whether I can get out of this one— whether Abba would allow me to go out, so far away, all by myself."

"Well, Sabah," Ravi said eagerly, "it might be far away in terms of distance, but I can tell you that it is safer there for a lone girl than it is in any of the cities in India. And, of course, I am there in case you have any problems."

Sabah turned slowly towards him, looking into his eyes, searching for something.

"Sabah! Bashir on the phone, asking for you," someone shouted across the room and broke the spell.

After that it was a madhouse of a day. The counting of votes had started and Bashir and Salima, who were part of the team of 'observers' representing KP on the spot, were periodically feeding back information on progress for different constituencies to Sabah at their office. The 'scoreboard' was soon filling up with the latest information. It was a see-saw battle through the day, but when counting was suspended for the day in the late evening, and Bashir and Salima came back to the KP office, they had happy expressions on their faces. Salima had a clear lead in her constituency, and so did a large number of their candidates in the fray. Indications were that though they would not get a clear majority, KP was liable to emerge as the party with the single largest number of candidates in the new Assembly. Their chances of being invited to form the government, along with support from some other party or legislators, were strong. Since Ravi was due to leave the next day before the final results came in, Bashir suggested that they have a small celebration in his honour before they all dispersed for the night.

An hour later everyone started getting ready to go home. It was already dark and getting chilly. Bashir offered to drop Ravi off to his house in his car. Salima had a vehicle at her disposal, the one she had been using for her campaigning, and she and Sabah would go off in that. They stood chatting for some time at the curb before Ravi got into the car; Salima excited and boisterous as usual, Sabah quiet and withdrawn. As Bashir started his car Sabah walked quickly away down the road, with a half wave of farewell over her shoulder, without looking back.

Ravi recalled Sabah's quiet demeanor throughout the later part of the evening, in contrast to the excitement that everyone else was displaying. It seemed as if she was alone, lost in her own thoughts, which seemed to overshadow the exuberance of impending victory. Was it because of the looming spectre of parting? Ravi too experienced a feeling of hollowness, of loss. As the aircraft began its descent at Delhi airport he wondered whether it was at all possible—whether either of them would have the courage to break through those gossamer threads of the last delicate barrier, the barrier of religion that stood between them.

Perhaps, as a first step, he would send those college brochures he had promised her. Then wait. There was a whole new world of promise, across the ocean.

ABOUT THE AUTHOR

Born in 1943. Graduated from St. Stephen's College, Delhi, in English Honours in 1964. Worked in various jobs in marketing and administration and as Trade Counsellor in the Royal Danish Embassy, New Delhi, where he was awarded the Queen's medal for meritorious service in 2005.

Has been actively involved in theatre since 1965, and has participated in all aspects of theatre. He won the Chaman Lal Memorial Society award for outstanding contribution to stage craft in 2003. He was drama critic for The Statesman newspaper for three years.

During his college days, and throughout his working life, he was writing poems and short stories in his spare time. On his retirement in 2010 he started compiling all his writings and devoting more time to creative writing. The result was the publishing of two books in 2012: *"The Revolution and other stories"**, a collection of short stories, and *"Little Matchsticks"**, a collection of poems. (*Google "Vinay Capila" for further information.)

The present book is his first effort at writing a full length novel. Though born and brought up in Delhi, a large part of the Author's psyche was formed in Kashmir, his mother's birthplace, which he visited innumerable times—from early childhood to graying maturity. He has witnessed the changing ethos of the terror stricken valley in its various phases.

Snippets from some of the author's recently published book of short stories:

"The Revolution and Other Stories", also available on Flipkart.

The Revolution: The slow deliberate voice of the emaciated man sent shivers down Ashok's spine. This was the end . . . . They had but one law: death to the traitor. He could not hope to escape . . . .

One Summer: I think back sometimes, of that first love . . . . And I wonder how one solitary moment that should have been so insignificant in a life span—can come like a raging fire and leave behind just charred, devastated silhouettes of regret.

Catch that Man: ". . . . You know sir, she killed our only child three months ago . . . . She sucked the poor fellows blood till he grew thin and frail—and eventually died . . . . I must go now—I must go and plunge this knife into her wicked breast . . . ."

The Idealist: Her lips moved fervently against his, seeking the peace that the turmoil in her brain needed. She wanted him to crush her, to make them one . . . .

The Last Post: They made their last stand about fifty meters away from their own lines. But before their troops could come to their rescue, the damage had been done. With safety sp much within their grasp, Captain Vikramjit

Singh saw with growing bitterness his two remaining companions falling to the hail of enemy bullets.

Vote for None: I suppose it was our youth, which closed our eyes to the writing on the wall and let us be beguiled by the endless promises that erupted like treacherous volcanoes during election times . . . .

Writer's Block: I scratched my beard . . . looking for inspiration . . . . Through the window a vaguely familiar film song floated in and spread itself across the room. And it came! Ah! Sweet inspiration! . . . A Hindi movie is like a mural . . . . Surely I could milk a few short stories out of one . . . .

> *"An arresting book of short stories by Vinay Capila, holds not only your attention but also your mind and heart . . . ."*
>
> **Dr. Kavita A. Sharma,**
> *educationist and published author.*